Theresa the Philosopher

Marquis d'Argens

Translated By Richard Robinson

&

The Carmelite Extern Nun

Anne-Gabriel Meusnier de Querlon

Translated By Richard Robinson

Sunny Lou Publishing Company
Portland, Oregon, USA
http://www.sunnyloupublishing.com

2nd Edition: February 24, 2024
Original Publication Date: April 25, 2021

ISBN: 978-1-955392-59-4

* * *

The translation of *Theresa the Philosopher* from French is based the "La Haye (A La Sphere) 1748-1910" edition of *Thérèse Philosophe.*

The translation of the *Carmelite Extern Nun* from French is based on the "A La Haye M. DCC. XLVII" (1747) edition of *Histoire de la Tourière des Carmelites*.

Contents

Forewords

Foreword to *Theresa the Philosopher*

The translator had a conversation once upon a time about *Theresa the Philosopher*, and he let slip how often he found himself laughing out loud while working on it. His erstwhile interlocutor was taken aback and asked point-blank: “What’s funny about it?” The translator was shocked and temporarily at a loss for words. It never occurred to him that somebody would not immediately find the novel funny. So he thought about it, long and hard, and this “foreword” is an effort to explain “what’s so funny about it.”

Theresa the Philosopher was written and published over 270 years ago – before the modern era, before the Napoleonic phenomenon, before the Directorate, before the French Revolution, and before the founding of the United States of America, for those of us on this side of the Atlantic. It’s a happy tale with a happy ending.

There was an even longer, early title for the book, typical of books of this period: *Theresa the Philosopher or Memoirs to Serve as an Aid to the Story of Father Dirrag and Mademoiselle Eradice, Together with the Story of Madame Bois-Laurier*. A mouthful, I’m sure you’ll agree.

Theresa the Philosopher (&c.) was published in 1748, which is around the time the modern novel was born. If we take Samuel Richardson's *Pamela*, published in 1740, as the first modern (albeit English) novel, where the characters are more than two-dimensional and the story depends more on what happens inside the mind of the characters than, say, where a boat might go (like *Robinson Crusoe* for example), *Pamela*, – or *Pamela; or Virtue Rewarded* (its longer title); or even *Pamela; or Virtue Rewarded In a Series of Familiar Letters from a Beautiful Young Damsel to her Parents* (longer still) – was a novel in the genre known as Conduct Literature. It told of a young (beautiful, of course) intelligent but virtuous girl, a domestic (of course), pursued amorously by her rakish lord and master, M. B***. The ambitious reader, after absorbing *Theresa the Philosopher*, and then *Pamela*, will see similarities.

The nexus, plexus, and decidedly sexus of literary correspondences, – including genre, theme, character, plot, period, title, character names ("M. B***" for instance), &c. – tacking back and forth and back again, across the English Channel, is enough to make Humbert Humbert's head, and Dolores Haze's tail, spin. In other words, for the millennials among us, there are lots of degrees of Kevin Bacon among the English and French literature of this period. The esteemed reader of any generation and any land mass is invited to do his or her own research on the subject. Here, we are merely trying to uncover and flesh out some of the more outstanding and protuberant connections and reverberations.

One of the more titillating connections is to the marquis de Sade's *Justine*, which was the novel he published in 1791, six years after publishing *The 120 Days of Sodom*, which latter novel (his first) he had written on (sadly appropriately) rolls of toilet paper, during his 3,650 days in the Bastille. *The 120 Days of Sodom* is a gloomy, depressing, and shocking piece of literature, and not very funny either if we remember it correctly. We mention it here to suggest only some corollaries, or nexuses, and to assist in putting *Theresa the Philosopher* in its proper place.

Justine is closer to *Theresa the Philosopher* than *120 Days of Sodom.* For one thing, *Justine* also had a longer title, true to the spirit of the period, and that was *Justine*, *or the Misfortunes of Virtue*, which reminds us of *Pamela*'s midriff-length title. Though *Justine* falls more into the category of Libertine Literature, than Conduct Literature. Like *Theresa the Philosopher*, which the French authorities of the time tried to track down and destroy, *Justine* was deemed an inappropriate guide of conduct for young French girls and, by edict of the government of Napoleon, copies were also ordered to be found and destroyed, if not burned at the stake. Yet they didn't find all the copies; its seemingly anonymous author (the marquis de Sade) was arrested and incarcerated at Charenton asylum for the insane for another 3,650 days plus two years, where he wrote and staged some plays, therapeutically.

The author of *Theresa the Philosopher* was also anonymous, and he went by the name of the marquis d'Argens.

So what are some of the corollaries with *Justine*? *Justine* is a young girl who goes by the name of Theresa; she does not write epistles, which is so utterly British, instead she recounts her story to a woman by the name of Madame de Lorsagne (who later turns out to be her sister, Juliette, in disguise, but that's not a corollary, but "Madame de C***" may be). As she falls into and out of and into again the hands of a series of rogues, rakes, rascals, and libertines, somewhere along the way she hooks up with a woman by the name of Mademoiselle DuBois. On reading *Theresa the Philosopher*, the attentive reader will see some plexuses and may come to believe that the infamous marquis was familiar with *Theresa the Philosopher* (as well as *Pamela*). The observant reader would be correct! According to one edition of *Theresa the Philosopher*, the one on which this translation is based, we find the following tidbit in the introduction to that work:

The marquis de Sade, in the Holland edition (1797) of the *New Justine* (t. VII, p. 97), states that the marquis d'Argens is the author of *Theresa the Philosopher*. "D'Argens (in his *Memoirs*, Paris edition, 1807, in-8, p. 304) had seen the most secret court proceedings of Father Girard and Cadière. De Sade, who belonged to an old aristocratic and clerical family from Provence, certainly knew d'Argens, who was from the same region."

And then there's this:

"… a charming performance from the pen of the Marquis d'Argens, alone to have discerned the possibilities of the genre, though only partially realizing them; alone to have achieved happy results from the combining of lust and impiety. These, speedily placed before the public, and in the shape the author had initially conceived them, finally gave us an idea of what an immoral book could be." —Donatien-Alphonse-François, the MARQUIS DE SADE

So the anonymous author of *Justine* was familiar with the very anonymous author of *Theresa the Philosopher* — attributed to Jean-Baptiste de Boyer (Marquis d'Argens). De Boyer also wrote and published several satirical novels, lending further weight to the humorous sections of *Theresa.*

Now that we know that *Theresa the Philosopher* is a novel in the Libertine tradition, the curious but impatient reader might ask – but why is it funny? Let's take a peek:

Long, fat, rubicund-headed penises pawned off as serpents that sting, lunge at, and shoot venom at little girls, especially those who want to make miracles. A whore who is also the eternal virgin because she has a congenital defect that prevents her maidenhead from being penetrated and who, not in spite of it, but quite frankly because of it, makes a pile of money in prostitution.

Three Capuchin monks so impossibly horny and rushing at a "fresh-looking girl" whom they can't fuck anyways, one of whom gets so drunk he vomits into the mouth of the sexagenarian procurer (DuBois), who vomits back again into his, just to even the score, before she pummels him with her fists. A flatulent-by-nature courtesan who hates sodomites so much that she eats a bunch of turnips before one arrives, and while he's inspecting her bunghole with a candle for two hours she finally lets out a big one, knocking him over and singeing his sideburns. A man so infatuated with music that, when making love, he gets hard with an aria in triple-time and soft by a flat note.

Are you thinking what we're thinking? Yes, this is Gargantua and Pantagruel territory. That "pentalogy of novels" – known more expansively as *The Life of Gargantua and of Pantagruel, or The Horrible and Terrifying Deeds and Words of the Very Renowned Pantagruel King of the Dipsodes, Son of the Great Giant Gargantua,* – is the great French satirical masterpiece, bar none (save *Theresa the Philosopher* maybe), a wildly bawdy and absurd novel written by François Rabelais and published in 1532.

There's more to a comedy, as a literary genre, than eliciting laughter however. It's not a comedy if the hero or heroine dies, for instance. Comedies have to end happily. *Theresa the Philosopher* is no exception. As often happens in a comedy, and particularly a romantic comedy, there is a bet, which everything depends on. It happens towards the end of the story. Her beau, the count, for whom she wrote her memoirs in the first place, bets her her maidenhead for a roomful of pornographic books and paintings, which she can't keep her eyes off of. If she can refrain from masturbating for two weeks, while surrounded by these books and paintings, she wins: the books and paintings are hers. If she can't, she loses: her maidenhead is his. She takes the bet and loses. But she wins too because she discovers that his serpent doesn't lunge at her or sting her, although it may shoot some venom at her, and that making love to the count is largely more satisfying than making love to her finger.

This most happy of endings makes the story a comedy, by definition.

It is for these reasons that the translator believes *Theresa the Philosopher* is more comedic than libertine in nature, that its libertinism was merely bait to attract readers and make some fast money, and that both the comedy and libertinism intertwined therein were intended to make the philosophy of the Enlightenment period a little easier to swallow. We hope that you will enjoy reading the story as much as we did translating it.

Foreword to *The Carmelite Extern Nun*

The immediate attraction, I imagine, for an 18th century reader of an erotic or libertine novella in general, – like *The Carmelite Extern Nun* – was the apparent scandal of finding religion and sex combined on the same page, in the same exhalation; it must have felt scandalous to see the sacred commingled with the profane, God and his priests or nuns defiled by sex.

Anticlericalism, antiestablishmentarianism, eroticism are all said to be the three main pillars or themes, sometimes even agendas, of the 18th century libertine novel. *Nun* offers up at least two of them for sale and lays them on the altar, so to speak: anticlericalism (indirectly) and eroticism (directly).

Both take front and center stage in *Nun.* Monks and nuns, back then particularly, but even today one imagines, were not supposed to be thought of as sexual animals. That's the nut of the scandal. They were, after all, supposed to have taken vows of chastity and acted angelically. Back "then" (which is really not so long ago temporally, I don't say morally, if you think about it), when the Catholic Church still had a strong hold on men's actions and beliefs, both in and out of the clergy – it was perfectly natural, even expected, for the average John or Mary Doe to be scandalized, outraged even, not merely by the idea, but by the suggestion, that priests or nuns engaged in sex. This taboo topic was possibly one reason for the huge popularity of libertine novels in the first place.

Of course, not all libertine novels mixed religion and sex. But the *The Carmelite Extern Nun* did, quite catholically, and so did several other important French libertine novels from the same period, *The Ecclesiastical Laurels* and *Theresa the Philosopher,* to name two, which makes three.

Today, in the 21st century, it is more common to visit a "genderless" restroom (as if anyone who visits it has no gender), check off on a government form what sex you had *at birth* (as if sex were a moveable trait, something like a moveable feast), and listen to a TV talk show host who is either gay or transgender or both – all *that* is more common today than attending church on Sundays, believing in God, or saying a prayer around the dinner table with the family – fifty years, nay, twenty years ago even. The original lure of an erotic or libertine novel today, consequently, cannot possess the same appeal as it did yesterday, – there is very little scandal in it, comparatively, all elements of the traditional libertine novel remaining the same. But nothing ever remains the same, things get better or they get worse. Taboo subjects are no different.

One element of *Nun* that is still taboo and shocking today is the element of incest, or presumed incest, which takes place briefly in one scene of the novella. It isn't absolutely clear whether incest really does take place however, even though there is a suggestion of it. The characters themselves aren't even quite sure. But they engage in it, or think they do, and quite scandalously that seems to arouse them.

Incest, as with bestiality, child pornography, and the lethal combination of sex and murder, are all probably now, as maybe they ever have been and should always be, the last frontiers in terms of shock value and scandal. We can only hope that things never go beyond this.

But enough of all this terrible scandal: let's come back up for some air now.

Besides scandal and anticlericalism, what else does *Nun* have in it that might be worthy of the modern reader's attention? The narrative is one thing.

The narrative, or the story-telling, in *Nun* is straight forward and moves at a rapid clip, which is invigorating. It is narration pure and simple, just like it was and just like it should be. A story is told, the story moves forward. It also happens to be libertine. It is almost like some prosaic version of a "bad" tale out of Chaucer. It is the story of a woman named Agnes, or Saint Nitouche, who is a nun in spite of herself, born of a prioress out of wedlock, a nun as well, and in spite of herself too; both of them are quite beautiful and possess an inordinate fund of sexual desire. (What a perfect combination for an erotic story!) Agnes engages in lots of sex over the course of her lifetime, with powerful men, and soon becomes a "kept" woman, which she takes enormous pride in, but which doesn't stop her from cheating on her man; later she has several boyfriends, and even a girlfriend (she becomes a furious tribade at one point in the novella), then finally she arrives at the very lucrative pinnacle of her career – she becomes a high-class procuress of her own bawdy house.

One thing that may strike a reader as particularly outstanding, possibly quaint, in all of this, but also so very modern, is the constant, almost bipolar, jumping back and forth between first-person and third-person narrators (by one and the same narrator). It is confusing, it is invigorating. At one moment it's Agnes did this, or Saint Nitouche (who is the same person) did that, and at the next moment, sometimes the next sentence or paragraph, it is "I" did this or this happened to "me." With the narrative's rapid pace, it works, in spite of the jumps, and arguably because of them. Some readers may find them confusing or annoying, at first: it is because we are not used to this sort of thing. But once you relax, and suspend your preconceived notions of what a narrator, or a narration, must be – you may find it perfectly natural and exhilarating; because it shows a very early and rich example of the novel form breaking the rigid bounds that have taken hold of it since the French Revolution and well into the Victorian Age and beyond, where the novelist is expected to assume one or another device or person and stick with it from beginning to end.

The last aspect of *Nun* that may strike the reader as curious and intriguing is just how similar it is to another novel that was published, right after it, – *Theresa the Philosopher*. Both novels were published in 1747 and 1748 respectively, so we are told. *Nun* is essentially *Theresa the Philosopher* published without the Enlightenment philosophy (and the flagellation). Or, to put it another way, it is Bois-Laurier's story in a nutshell, in its primordial form (from *Theresa the Philosopher)*. Although many of Agnes' personality traits and life events find themselves echoed later in the character and events of Bois-Laurier, – some of her character and life events spill over and onto, and get shared with, Thérèse as well, in the latter novel. Which is fascinating to watch.

Here is a short list of some of the more striking examples of this:

- Agnes' face gets pummeled and disfigured toward the end of her story, effectively ending her successful career as a prostitute and procuress. Bois-Laurier's face is marred by small pox, making her unrecognizable, immediately after her successful career as a prostitute.

- Agnes eavesdrops and spies on her mum, the prioress, and a chaplain, her confessor, having sex in a chair. Thérèse eavesdrops on Mme C***, a friend of her mother's, and Abbot T***, her confessor, as they make love and philosophize in a bower or on Mme C***'s divan.

- Agnes is a high-class prostitute; so is Bois-Laurier. Both are very successful at it and make a great deal of money at their "profession."

- Agnes is naïve, or affects to be (that's why she's nicknamed Saint Nitouche); so is Thérèse, without the affectation, but with some of the same duplicity.

- Agnes actually enjoys sex, unlike many of the sadder, low-class prostitutes she sees huddling under the arches; she chose her profession (just as much as it chose her); Thérèse enjoys sex from a very early age, masturbating in her sleep, as early as 5 or 6 years old.

- The sex scene between Agnes' mother, the prioress, and her lover the chaplain are echoed in scenes between Mme C*** and Abbot T*** in the second section of *Theresa the Philosopher*.

Looking over this list, it may not come as a surprise to the avid reader who devours both *Theresa the Philosopher* and *Nun,* that Thérèse herself reads, at the end of her own story, among other licentious tracts, none other than *The Carmelite Extern Nun.*

– *Richard Robinson*

Theresa the Philosopher

Or Memoirs to Serve as an Aid to the Story of Father Dirrag and Mademoiselle Eradice, Together with the Story of Madame Bois-Laurier

Marquis d'Argens

Introduction

The very notorious trial of Catherine Cadière against Father Girard has provided the pretext for re-publication of this work.

Father Jean-Baptiste Gérard [sic], a French Jesuit preacher, was named, in or around 1728, rector of the royal seminary at the port of Toulon. There, one of his penitents, the eighteen-year-old Catherine Cadière, a great beauty from a good family, attached herself to him with a mystical exaltation fomented by her reading, imprudently, several books on asceticism: she claimed to be the object of all sorts of miracles. Father Girard encouraged her down this dangerous path from the start; but soon, after she had caught on to his deception, he recused himself. The young lady, stung by his abandonment, confided in the prior at the convent of the Carmelites, a fervent Jansenist and a great enemy of the Jesuits. This religious man made her repeat her accusations before witnesses. The Jesuits succeeded subsequently in having the young Cadière locked up in the Ursulines. This abuse of authority was their undoing. The affair was brought before the Parliament at Aix, where Catherine Cadière accused Father Girard of seduction, spiritual incest, magic, and sorcery. After long and torturous debates, Father Girard's case was thrown out of court by a margin of one vote: of the twenty-five judges, twelve had condemned him to being burned alive. Public opinion had furthermore openly taken sides against him; he had to quit Toulon in secret. He went to Lyon, and from there to Dôle, where he died two years later, on July 4, 1733.[1]

The trial had a considerable impact. The factums, anti-factums, instructive memoirs, observations, demonstrations, etc., written on this occasion are many and voluminous. They would be worthy, doubtless, of a close examination, possibly even a precise study. Those in the National Library's possession comprise, in the catalog of factums put together by A. Corda in 1890, sixty-nine titles, whose captions take up nearly forty columns in the catalog.

A curious allusion to this affair was found in a brochure published in 1733 under the title ANECDOTES TO SERVE AS AN AID TO THE SECRET STORY OF THE EBUGORS, which attacked, under a thin veil of easily decipherable anagrams, the vice of sodomy. Mademoiselle Cadière became *Calederia*; Father Girard was called *Ripergader* and is the leader of the *Caginiens* [Ignatiens or Jesuits]. This latter group, faithful adepts of the *Ebugors* (buggers or sodomites) reproached *Ripergader*, their leader, for having let himself fall for the charms of *Calederia*, a Cytherean. But the guilty party, after serving a light sentence, returned to his first passions.[2]

A little poem by the libertine Robbé de Beauveset has celebrated also, maliciously, Cadière's stigmata and Father Girard's ecstasies:

---

[1]Original footnote: See *J.-F. Barbler's Journal*, August, September, October, 1731.

[2]Original footnote: See *Anecdotes to Assist in the Secret History of the Ebugors*, ch. XXI, pp. 109 ff.

QUIETISTIC ECSTASY

One morning while at a distance
The good Father Girard
Stigmatized Sister Cadière,
A young extern sister showed up,
Who remained for some time in admiration
At the sight of so novel an operation;
Because she was said to be virgin,
Very ignorant in bagatelles.
Whatever the case, wishing to get a good look,
With unsure step, she quietly approaches;
She examines, and not long afterwards,
Behold our two devotees fallen into a swoon.
The innocent sister, believing they were dying,
Was particularly concerned for the good Father;
And, attempting to succor him,
Wanted him to drink a little vulnerary liquid.
The hypocrite was enraged she'd seen the mystery;
But trusting in her simplicity,
He looked at her severely.
"Go away, my sister," he said with emphasis;
"Go away, we are in ecstasy."[3]

* * *

THERESA THE PHILOSOPHER used several anagrams, but they were very thinly veiled: *Dirrag*, Girard; *Eradice*, Cadière; *Vencerop*, Provence; *Volnot*, Toulon.

* * *

THERESA THE PHILOSOPHER, OR MEMOIRS TO SERVE AS

[3]Original footnote: *The Light-hearted Works of Robbé Beauveset.* London, 1901, tome I, p. 4.

AN AID TO THE STORY OF SPIRITUAL DIRECTOR DIRRAG AND MADEMOISELLE ERADICE (of Father Girard and the young lady Cadière), TOGETHER WITH THE STORY OF MADAME BOIS-LAURIER. The Hague (at the Sphere), s. d. (1748), 2 parts in 1 illustrated vol. of 16 uncensored prints included with the volume.

The re-printings of this work were quite numerous and always accompanied by illustrations that were too explicit to be made public. Such is the madness of lecherous attitudes and the artificial excitement obtained from a drawing. To list said publications here would be tiresome; they can be found at great length in the *Bibliography* of the Countess de I***, tome III, col. 1211-1213.

The author of this work is perhaps d'Arles de Montigny, War Commissioner; he was suspected of it and passed eight months in the Bastille on account of it. The marquis de Sade, in the Holland edition (1797) of the *New Justine* (t. VII, p. 97), states that the marquis d'Argens is the author of *Theresa the Philosopher.* "D'Argens (in his *Memoirs*, Paris edition, 1807, in-8, p. 304) had seen the most secret court proceedings of Father Girard and Cadière. De Sade, who belonged to an old aristocratic and clerical family from Provence, certainly knew d'Argens, who was from the same region."[4]

The first edition, published clandestinely, was sought out assiduously by the police. Published reports in the *Archives of the Bastille* (t. XII, pp. 299-344) often speak of inquiries, legal proceedings,

[4]Original footnote: See the *Bibliography* of Countess d'I***.

seizures on the subject of this unfortunate novel. The Jesuits, still powerful, were too dangerous to be touched: their glib, passionate morality was too seductive.

Theresa the Philosopher

What's that, sir! seriously, you want me to write down my story? You want me to give an account of the mystical scenes that took place between Mademoiselle Eradice and the Very Reverend Father Dirrag; you want me to tell you about the adventures of Madame C*** with the abbot T***? From a girl who has never written anything before, you ask for details that require a "certain presentation of the materials"? You desire a painting where the scenes I have described to you, or those we've been actors in, lose nothing of their lasciviousness; that the metaphysical reasonings retain their energy? In all honesty, my dear count, that seems beyond my abilities. Besides, Eradice was my friend; Father Dirrag was my spiritual director; I have feelings of gratitude for Madame C*** and abbot T***. Will I betray the trust of people I owe so much to, because of the actions of the former and the wise reflections of the latter, who gradually opened my eyes to the prejudices of my youth? But, you say, if the example and the reasonings have given you happiness, why not try to contribute to the happiness of others in the same way, by example and by reasonings? Why be afraid to write down truths that might be useful for the good of society? Well, my dear benefactor, I can no longer resist: let's write; my ingenuity will need to make up for the absence of a refined style, as far as thoughtful readers are concerned, and I have no fear of sots. No, your tender Thérèse will never refuse you; you will see all the twists and turns of her heart, from her most tender childhood; her soul in its entirety will unfold before you with the details of the little adventures that led her, in spite of herself, step by step, to the pinnacle of sexual delight.

Imbecilic mortals! you think you're masters of snuffing out the passions that nature has put in you! They're the work of God. You want to destroy them, these passions, and keep them within certain limits. Madmen! Do you pretend in this way to be second creators more powerful than the first? Will you never see that all is as it should be, and that all in life is good; that all is from God, nothing from you, and that it is as difficult to create a thought as it is to create an arm or an eye?

The course of my life is an incontestable proof of these truths. From my most tender childhood, all I heard was talk about the love of virtue and the horror of vice. "You will not be happy," they told me, "unless you practice Christian virtues and morality. Everything that strays from these is vice; vice attracts contempt, contempt engenders shame and remorse, which follow by necessity." Persuaded by the soundness of these lessons, I sought in good faith, until twenty-five years old, to act according to these precepts; we will see just how well I succeeded.

I was born in the province of Vencerop. My father was a good bourgeois, a merchant from..., a pretty little town, where everything inspires joy and pleasure; gallantry seems to make up the sole interest of society there. There, one loves from the moment one begins to think, and one thinks only to facilitate the means by which to enjoy love's sweetness. My mother, who was from..., added to the active minds of the women of this province, which bordered on Vencerop, the happy temperament of a Venceropalian sensualist. My father and my mother lived with economic restraint, counting their pennies, getting by on a modest income and what their small business produced. Their labors were unable to change the state of their fortune: my father supported a young widow, a merchant in his neighborhood, his mistress; my mother was supported by her lover, an exceptionally rich gentleman, who had the kindness of honoring my father with his friendship. Everything proceeded with admirable orderliness; one knew what to expect, what was what, and never has a marriage seemed more together.

After ten years had passed in so laudable an arrangement, my mother became pregnant: she gave birth to me. My birth incommoded her maybe more terribly than death itself would have. Her efforts, during childbirth, caused a rupture in her that made it sadly necessary for her to renounce forever the pleasures that had brought me into existence.

Everything changed at home. My mother became devout, the Father Superior of the Capuchins took over the assiduous visits of M. the marquis de ***, who was sent packing. My mother's stock of feelings hadn't changed, only their object had: she gave to God, by necessity, what she had previously given to the marquis by taste and temperament.

My father passed away and left me while I was still in the cradle. My mother, I don't know why, moved to Volnot, a famous port town. From the most gallant lady in the world she turned into the wisest and perhaps most virtuous woman that ever existed.

I was just seven years old when this loving mother, always concerned for my health and my education, noticed that I was losing weight substantially; a skilled physician was called in to consult on my illness; I had a voracious appetite, no fever; I felt no pain; but I was listless, and my legs no longer held me up. Fearful for my days, my mother never quit my side and had me sleep with her in bed. Imagine her surprise one night when, seeing me asleep, she noticed that I had placed my hand on that part of my body that distinguishes girls from boys, where by a benign rubbing I procured for myself a pleasure seldom known to a girl seven years old but very common to a girl fifteen. My mother could hardly believe her eyes. She gently lifts the blanket and the sheet, and, prudent and knowledgeable woman that she is, she waits faithfully for the denouement of my action. As was to be expected: I got excited, I quivered, and the pleasure woke me up.

My mother's first response was to scold me in a big way; she asked me where I had learned the horrors she had just witnessed. With tears running down my cheeks, I told her that I had no idea what I had done to upset her; that I didn't know what she meant by such things as *unseemly fondling*, *shamelessness*, and *mortal sin*. The naivety of my responses convinced her of my innocence, and I went back to sleep; new ticklings for me, new reprimands by my mother. Finally, after several nights of attentive observation, my mother no longer had any doubt in her mind that it was the strength of sexual desire that made me do, while sleeping, what so many poor monks and nuns do while awake, to relieve themselves. She decided to bind my hands, so that it would be impossible for me to continue my nocturnal amusements.

I soon recovered my health and my original vigor. The habit was lost, but my sexual desire increased. At nine years old, I felt anxieties and desires for something I had no idea where it led. Several girls and boys my own age got together often in the attic or in some out-of-the-way room. There, we played little games: one of the boys was elected school master, and the least mistake was punished by a whipping. The boys pulled down their pants, the girls hitched up their skirts and blouses, while everyone looked on attentively; you would have seen five or six little butts admired, caressed, and whipped one after the other. What we called the boys' *wee-wee* served as our plaything; we passed our hands over it a hundred times, again and again; we squeezed it; we made it our puppet; we kissed this little instrument, which we were so ignorant of in terms of its purpose and worth; our little butts were kissed in turn: the center of pleasure alone was neglected; why is that? I have no idea; but such were our games; simple Nature dictated them to us, I'm merely reporting what I know here.

After two years of this innocent libertinage, my mother sent me to a nunnery: I was about eleven years old then. The Mother Superior's first concern was to have me make my first Confession. I presented myself before this tribunal without fear because I had no remorse. I let it all out before the old guardian of the Capuchins, my mother's director of conscience, who listened to me, all the trifles and peccadillos of a girl my age. After having accused me of faults that I believed myself guilty of: "You will be a saint some day," this good Father told me, "if you continue to follow, as you have done, the principles of virtue that your mother inspires in you; at all costs, do not listen to the demon of the flesh; I am your mother's confessor; she alarmed me as to the pleasure she believes you take in impurity, that most infamous of vices; I am delighted to say that she was mistaken in her ideas as to what she thought your illness of four years ago was; but if it wasn't for her concern, my dear child, you would have been damned for all eternity, in both body and soul. Yes, I am sure of it, presently, that when she caught you touching yourself, you were not doing it voluntarily, and I am convinced that she is mistaken in her conclusions as to your salvation."

Alarmed at what my confessor was saying, I asked him what I had done that gave my mother so bad an impression of myself. He was quick to tell me, in no uncertain terms, what had happened and the efforts that my mother had taken to correct me of a defect that he wished, he said, I would never know the consequences of.

These reflections made me think immediately of our games in the attic, which I just spoke about. My face turned red, I lowered my eyes, like a shameful person, forbidden, and I thought I perceived, for the first time in my life, the crime in our pleasure. The Father asked me why I had fallen silent and why I was sad; I told him everything. He demanded such details from me! My naivety on the terms, attitudes, and kinds of pleasure I admitted to persuaded him even more of my innocence. He blamed those games with a prudence that is uncommon in Church ministers; but his expressions were enough to show me the idea he had of my sexual desire. Fasting, prayer, meditation, a hair-shirt were the weapons he prescribed for me to do battle with my passions.

"Keep your hands" he said to me, "and your eyes off that vile part of the body where you piss; it is none other than the apple that seduced Adam and caused the damnation of the human species through original sin; it is inhabited by the devil, it is where he lays his hat, it is his throne; do not let yourself be caught off guard by this enemy of God and men. Nature will soon cover over that part of your body with a nasty fur, just like what wild beasts are covered with, to mark, by this punishment, the shame, obscurity, and forgetfulness that must be his share. Take even more precaution with that bit of flesh the young men your same age have, which was your plaything in the attic: it is the serpent, my dear girl, the same that tempted Eve, our common mother. Let neither your eyes nor your hands be soiled by that villainous beast: it would sting you and devour you, infallibly, sooner or later."

"What! how can that be possible, Father," I responded emotionally, "that it's a serpent and that it's as dangerous as you say! Gosh! It seemed so docile to me! it didn't bite any of my companions; I can assure you it has a very small mouth and no teeth, I got a good look at it..."

"Come on, child," said my confessor, interrupting me, "trust me: the serpents you had the recklessness to touch were too young, too small as yet to cause the evil they are capable of; but they will get longer, they will get fatter, they will lunge at you, and it is then when you must fear the effect of their venom, which they are accustomed to shoot at you with a kind of fury, and which will poison you, body and soul."

Finally, after more lessons of this sort, the good Father dismissed me, leaving me strangely perplexed. I retired to my room, my imagination struck by what I had just heard, but much more affected by the idea of the lovable serpent than by that of the remonstrances and threats I had received on the subject. All the same, I practiced in good faith what I had promised; I resisted the efforts of my sexual desire and I became an example of virtue.

How many struggles, my dear count, I had to go through until the age of twenty-five, when my mother pulled me out of that cursed convent! I was barely sixteen years old when I fell into a state of listless indolence and inertia which was the fruit of my meditations; they made me see two passions physically inside me, which I found impossible to reconcile. On the one hand, I loved God with good faith, and I wanted with all my heart to serve him in the way I was told he wanted to be served. On the other hand, I felt strong sexual desires that I was unable to disentangle the purpose of. That charming serpent constantly primped himself within my soul and planted himself there in spite of myself, while I was awake and while I was sleeping. Sometimes, deeply moved, I thought about reaching forward with my hand and caressing him, I admired his noble, haughty smile, his resoluteness, although I was still ignorant of his purpose; my heart beat at a surprising rate, and, carried away by the force of my ecstasy or my dream, always characterized by a shivering sensual delight, I hardly knew myself anymore, my hand laid hold of the apple, and my finger imitated the serpent.

Turned on by those forerunners of pleasure, I was incapable of any other thought; even if hell had opened up before my eyes, I would have been unable to stop, threats of remorse were powerless over me! The cup of sensual delight overflowed, and my sensual acts exceeded all measure.

The troubles that followed! fasting, hair-shirt, meditation were my lot: I broke down into tears. To be honest, those remedies, by upsetting my system, by derailing my machine, healed me instantly of my passion; but they altogether ruined my temperament and my health; in the end, I sank into a state of listlessness that was pulling me visibly to the grave, until my mother pulled me out of the convent.

Tell me, crafty or ignorant theologians who invent our crimes as you see fit: what was it that instilled in me the two passions I struggled with – *love of God* and *love of pleasure in the flesh*? Was it Nature or was it the Devil? You choose. But would you dare propose that one or the other is more powerful than God? If they are subordinate to him, then God must have allowed those passions to reside within me: it was his doing. But, you will reply, God gave you reason in order to become enlightened. Yes, but not to decide. Reason had allowed me to recognize the two passions that stirred within me: it's because of reason that I realized consequently that, having received everything from God, I received from him also these two passions with all their force; but this same reason that enlightened me didn't decide anything. However, you will continue, God made you mistress of your willpower, made you free to choose between good and evil. A mere game of words. This willpower and this pretended freedom have the strength only, and act only, in reaction to the strength of the passions or appetites that entice us. For example, I seem free to kill myself, or to throw myself out the window. Not at all: because the desire to live is stronger in me than the desire to die, I would never kill myself. Such a person, you will say, is sufficiently master of himself to be able to reach into his pocket and give one hundred *louis d'or* to the poor or to his indulgent confessor. He is not at all able: because the desire to keep his money is much stronger than that of obtaining a useless absolution for his sins, and he will necessarily hold on to his money. Finally, each man can demonstrate for himself that reason serves only to let him know how strongly he should desire or avoid such and such a thing, combined with the pleasure or displeasure he would receive from it. From this knowledge acquired by reason results what we call *will* and *determination*. But this will and this determination are precisely subject to the strength of the passion or desire acting on us, just as a four-pound weight determines necessarily which side of a balance will drop when the other pan contains only two pounds.

But, a quibbler who sees only the outside of things will say in response, am I not free to drink a bottle of Burgundy or Champagne with my dinner? Am I not able to choose whether to stroll along the promenade of the Tuileries or through the Terrasse des Feuillants?

I admit that whenever the soul is perfectly indifferent as to its determination, when the desire to do this or that are held in equal balance, in just equilibrium, we cannot perceive this lack of freedom to choose; it's far off in the distance where we no longer discern objects; but as soon as we get closer to these objects, we distinctly perceive the underlying mechanism of our actions in life, and when we recognize it happening in one case, we recognize it happening in all cases, for Nature acts in all cases by the same principle.

Our quibbler sits down at the table, and he is served oysters; the oysters determine him to choose Champagne with his meal. But someone will say he was free to choose Burgundy. I say no: it's quite true that another motive, another desire stronger than the first could determine him to drink the Burgundy instead: well, in that case, this last desire would equally constrain his supposed freedom.

Our same quibbler, upon entering the promenade of the Tuileries, notices a pretty woman of his acquaintance on the Terrasse des Feuillants; he decides to join her, unless some other reason of interest or pleasure leads him away. But whatever he chooses to do, there will always be a reason, a desire, that determines him invincibly to do one thing or another, which will constrain his will.

To admit that man is free, it would be necessary to suppose that he determines his actions on his own; but if he's influenced by various degrees of passion whose nature or feelings affect him, then he's not free; a certain degree of more or less active desire decides him just as invincibly as a weight of four pounds is heavier than three.

I ask my interlocutor again to tell me what it is that prevents him from thinking like me on the matter at hand, and why I cannot determine myself to think like him on this matter. He will respond doubtless that his ideas, his notions, his feelings constrain him to think as he does. But from this reflection that demonstrates to him internally that he is not master of himself to will to think like me, nor I like him, it necessarily follows that we are not free to think however we decide. Now, if we are not free to think, how could we be free to act, for thought is the cause, and action is nothing but the effect; and how can an effect be *free* of a cause that is itself not *free*? That implies a contradiction.

To succeed in convincing ourselves of this truth, let's shine the light of experience on it. Gregory, Damon, and Philinte are three brothers who were raised by the same masters until the age of twenty-five; they have never left each other's side, and they have received the same education, the same lessons in morality and religion. However Gregory loves wine, Damon loves women, and Philinte is devout. What is it that determined the three different wills of these three brothers? It can be neither the acquisition nor the knowledge of good and evil, for they all received the same precepts by the same masters: each one of them has therefore within himself different principles, different passions, that have decided their diverse wills, in spite of the uniformity of their acquired knowledge. I will go further: Gregory, who loves wine, was the most honest and sociable person, the best of friends, when he hadn't been drinking, but from the moment he acquired a taste for this enchanting liquor, he became a liar, a calumniator, a quarreler, he would have slit his own throat for the pleasure he takes in the company of his best friend. Now, was Gregory master of this change of will that happened so suddenly in him? No, certainly not, because in a normal state of mind he detested the actions he had been forced to commit while under the influence. Some idiots however would admire Gregory's continence because he didn't love running after skirts; others would admire Damon's sobriety because he didn't love drinking wine; others still would admire Philinte's piety because he loved neither women nor wine, but he enjoyed a similar pleasure as a result of his inclination to devotion. It's in this way that the majority of men are duped by the idea that they possess human virtues or vices.

I will conclude. The arrangement of the organs, the disposition of the fibers, a certain movement in the fluids determine the type of passions; the various degrees of strength by which they act on us constrain the reason, determining the will in the greatest actions in our life. It's this that makes a passionate man, a wise man, a fool. The fool is no less free than the other two, for he acts by the same principles; nature is consistent. To suppose that a man is free and that he decides for himself is to make him God's equal.

Now back to my story. I said that when I was twenty years old my mother pulled me out of the convent nearly dead. My entire system was languishing, my skin had a yellow hue to it, my eyes were livid: I looked like a walking skeleton. In short, devotion was going to make me kill myself, until I returned to my mother's home. An expert physician, who visited the convent on his own initiative, understood from the beginning the principal cause of my illness. That divine essence, which procures for us the one physical pleasure, the only one that is not bitter to the taste, the dispersal and flow of which is as necessary, I say, for certain temperaments as what results from the food that nourishes us, had flowed from vessels suitable to it into others foreign to it; it was this that had thrown my entire system out of whack.

My mother was advised to find me a husband, as the only remedy that could save my life. She spoke with me about it gently, but, taken up as I was with my own prejudices, I told her, without mincing words, that I would rather die than displease God by so miserable a state of affairs, which He would tolerate only because of his great goodness. No matter what she said, I could not be moved; my weakened nature left me no sort of desire in this world; I could envision only the goodness that had been promised to me in the next life.

I continued my pious practices with all imaginable fury. I had often heard people speak of the famous Father Dirrag; I wanted to see him; he became my spiritual director; and Mademoiselle Eradice, his most tender penitent, was soon my best friend.

You are familiar, my dear count, with the story of those two infamous individuals; I will not try to repeat for you all that the public knows and says about them; but an unusual anecdote, which I was witness to, might amuse you and serve to convince you that, if it is true that Mademoiselle Eradice knew full well what she was about when she finally reciprocated the embraces of that hypocrite, it is at least certain that she was the dupe of his holy lubricity for a long time before then.

Mademoiselle Eradice had taken to me with the most tender of friendships; she confided in me her most intimate secrets; the similarity of mood, pious practice, and even perhaps temperament that existed between us made us inseparable. Being both of us virtuous, our dominant passion was to acquire the reputation for being saintly with an inordinate desire to make miracles. That passion dominated her so powerfully that she would have suffered, with a constancy worthy of martyrs, all imaginable torments, if she could be persuaded that in so doing she could make a second Lazarus rise from the dead; Father Dirrag possessed, more than anyone, the talent to make her believe what she wanted.

Eradice had told me on multiple occasions, with a kind of vanity, that this father spoke his mind with her alone; that in the particular conversations they often had together in her room, he assured her that she was "this close" to becoming a saint; that

God had revealed it to him in a dream, by which he had understood clearly that she was on the verge of making the greatest of miracles, if only she continued to let herself be led through the necessary stages of virtue and mortification.

Jealousy and envy come in all shapes and sizes; a devout person perhaps is the most susceptible to them.

Eradice perceived that I was jealous of her happiness and even that I seemed to put no stock in what she confided in me. Actually, what I betrayed to her was the surprise I felt when she told me about her special conversations with Father Dirrag, who had always avoided having similar conversations with me, at the home of one of his other penitents, my friend, who was stigmatized, just like Eradice. Doubtless, my sad face and yellow complexion did not seem to the Reverend Father the proper restorative for exciting the desire he needed for his spiritual labors. I got caught up in the game: boo hoo! no stigmata, no special conversations for me! All bent out of shape, I pretended not to believe a word she was telling me.

Visibly moved, Eradice offered to make me, the following day, an eye witness to her happiness. "You'll see," she told me with warmth, "the strength of my spiritual exercises, through what stages of penitence the good Father leads me on my way to becoming a great saint, and you'll have no doubt about my ecstasies, my raptures, which are a consequence of these same exercises. Let my example, my dear Thérèse," she added while lowering her voice again, "have on you, as a first miracle, the effect of detaching your mind entirely from matter by virtue of meditation, that you might place them both in God alone!"

I showed up the following day, at five o'clock in the morning, at Eradice's place, as agreed. I found her in prayer, a book in hand. "The holy man's about to arrive," she told me, "and God with him: hide yourself in this little room, where you can hear and see as much of God's bounty as He wants to reveal, in favor of his vile creature, by the pious attentions of our director of conscience." A moment later, someone knocked on the door softly. I hid in the little room that Eradice locked me in. A hole as large as a hand in the door to that little room, covered by old wallpaper from Bergamo and very transparent, allowed me to see clearly into the room in its entirety, without risk of being seen.

The good Father entered. "Bonjour, my dear sister in God," he said. "May the Holy Spirit and St. Francis be with you!" She threw herself down at his feet, but he pulled her up again and had her sit down next to him. "It is necessary," the holy man said to her, "that I repeat for you the principles that should guide you in all your actions in life; but first tell me about your stigmata; the one you have on your chest, is it still in the same condition? Let me see it." Eradice began dutifully to uncover her left tit, which was above the stigma. "Oh! sister, stop: cover your breast with this handkerchief." (He hands her one.) "Such things are not meant for a member of our society: I only need to see the wound that St. Francis has imprinted on you. Ah! it is still there. Good," he said, "I am content. St. Francis still loves you: the wound is bright red and pure; I made it a point to bring with me again his holy bit of cord; we will need it at the end of our exercises. I have said it before, my sister," he continued, "that you distinguish yourself from my other penitents, your companions, for I see that God distinguishes you from his holy flock, like the sun distinguishes itself from the moon and other planets. It is for this reason that I am not afraid to reveal to you his most hidden mysteries. I have said it before, my dear sister, *forget yourself* and *let be what will be*. God wants only our heart and soul. It is by forgetting the body that we arrive at union with God, at becoming a saint, at making miracles. I cannot hide from you, my little angel, that in our last exercise together, I felt that your spirit still clung to the flesh. What! can you not, in part, imitate those blessed martyrs, who were flagellated, tormented, roasted, without suffering the least pain, because their mind was so occupied with God's glory, who had within themselves not one particle of spirit that was not used to this end? It is a certain mechanism, my dear girl: we feel and we have no idea what is good or bad physically, nor what is good or bad mentally, save through the senses.

"From the moment we touch, hear, see, *et cetera*, an object, particles of spirit flow into the cavities of the nerves and then go and alert the soul. If you possess enough fervor to reassemble, by strength of meditation on the love you owe God, all the particles of spirit within you, by applying themselves to this object, it is certain that not a single one of them will remain to alert the soul of the blows to your flesh: you simply will not feel them. Look at the hunter, his mind occupied with tracking down the game he pursues, he feels neither the brambles nor the thorns that tear at his flesh as he runs through the forest. Weaker than him, focused on an object a thousand times more interesting, will you feel the feeble blows of discipline if your soul is completely occupied with the happiness you expect? Such is the touchstone that leads us on to make miracles; such ought to be the state of perfection that unites us with God...

"We are going to begin now, my dear girl: do your duty well, and you can be sure that with the help of the cord of St. Francis and your meditation, this pious exercise will finish in a torrent of inexpressible delights. Get down on your knees, my child, and discover those parts of your flesh that are the reasons for God's anger: the mortification they will experience will unite your mind intimately with Him. I will say it again, forget yourself and *let be what will be*."

Mademoiselle Eradice obeyed him immediately without another word. She knelt down on the prie-dieu, with a book in front of her; then, lifting her skirts and her shirt up over her waist, she uncovered her two buns, white as snow and each perfectly oval, held up by two thighs of admirable proportion. "Lift your shirt higher," he said: "it is not good; there, just like that. Now join your hands together and lift your soul to God; fill your mind with the idea of the eternal happiness that has been promised to you." Then the Father drew near to a stool on which he got down on his knees behind her and a little to the side of her. Beneath his robe, which he pulled up and tucked into his belt, was a large and long handful of birch rods, which he presented to his penitent to kiss.

Glued to the events of the scene unfolding before me, I was filled with holy horror; I experienced a kind of shuddering that I cannot describe. Eradice didn't say a word. The Father took in, with his eyes filled with fire, the buns that were before him; and as he kept his eyes fixed on her, I heard him say in a whisper, with a tone of admiration: "Ah! what beautiful breasts! What charming tits!" Then he bent down, and got up again, at intervals, murmuring some verses; nothing escaped his lubricity. After several minutes, he asked his penitent if her soul had entered into contemplation. "Yes, my Very Reverend Father," she said; "I feel my spirit detaching itself from my flesh, and I beg you to begin the sacred work."

"That will do," responded the Father, "your spirit will be content." He recited some more prayers, and the ceremony began by three blows with the birch rods that he applied rather lightly to her buttocks. These three blows were followed by another verse that he recited, and successively three more blows with the birch rods, a little stronger this time.

After five or six verses recited and interrupted by this sort of diversion, imagine my surprise when I see Father Dirrag unbuttoning his trousers, pulling out an inflamed shaft similar to that fatal serpent that my former spiritual director had reproached me for! This monster had grown to a length, a fatness, and a hardness foretold by the Capuchin; it made me shiver. Its rubicund head seemed to be menacing Eradice's buns, which had become a most beautiful crimson color; the Father's face was all afire. "You should now be," he said, "in the most perfect state of contemplation: your soul must be detached from your senses. If my girl does not disappoint my holy hopes, she will no longer see, hear, or feel."

At this moment, the executioner let fall a hail-storm of blows on all parts of Eradice's uncovered body. But she didn't say a word, she remained un-moved, insensible to these terrible blows, and I no-ticed merely a convulsive movement of her buttocks, which tightened and relaxed repeatedly. "I am happy with you," he said after a quarter of an hour of this cruel discipline; "now it is time to begin enjoying the fruit of your holy labor; do not listen to me, my dear girl, but let yourself be taken: put your face down on the floor: with the venerable cord of St. Francis, I am going to chase out of you all that remains impure."

The good Father placed her actually in a most humiliating position, but also one that was most suit-able to his purpose. Never had she looked more beau-tiful; her ass was half-exposed, and one could see the two paths of pleasure in their entirety.

After a moment of contemplation, the hyp-ocrite moistened with his saliva what he called the "cord," and while uttering some words in a tone of voice that sounded like the exorcism of a priest labor-ing to expel the devil out of the body of a demoniac, His Reverence began his intromission.

I was in a position to observe every little de-tail of this scene; the windows of the room where it took place were opposite the door of the small room I found myself in. Eradice had just gotten back onto her knees on the floor, her arms crossed on top of her prie-dieu, and her head resting on her arms; with her shirt carefully raised to her waist, I could see, in a half profile, her admirable buns and ass. This obscene perspective attracted the fixed attention of the Very Reverend Father, who got down on his knees himself, with the legs of his penitent between his own, his trousers down, his terrible cord in hand, mumbling some words that I could hardly hear.

He stayed in this edifying position for several moments, observing the altar with his enflamed eyes, and seeming undecided on the nature of the sacrifice he was going to offer. Two orifices presented themselves to him, he devoured them with his eyes, unsure of his choice: the one was a delectable morsel for a man of his robe, but he had promised his penitent pleasure and ecstasy; what to do? He dared to direct the head of his instrument several times into his preferred path which he penetrated lightly; but finally prudence got the better of pleasure, I owe him that. I distinctly saw His Reverence's bright red phallus enter the canonical way, after having delicately, partially, opened her vermillion lips with the thumb and forefinger of both hands.

This work was begun with three vigorous thrusts that penetrated her nearly half-way; then, suddenly, the Father's apparent calm turned into a kind of fury. What a look on his face! My God! Imagine for yourself a satyr, lips covered in foam, mouth open, gnashing his teeth sometimes, puffing and panting like a bellowing bull: his nostrils were flared and agitated; he kept his hands raised by their four fingers on Eradice's croup; it was clear that he wasn't placing them there for support; his spread fingers were in convulsion, and they assumed the shape of a roast capon's claws. His head was lowered and his gleaming eyes were fixed on the work performed by his linchpin, whose ins and outs he watched while, when in reverse motion, it did not exit the sheaf, and while, with each forward thrust, his stomach did not touch the belly of the penitent, who, if she had turned her head around, would have been able to divine whom the pretended cord belonged to. What presence of mind!

I saw that about one inch of the holy instrument was constantly kept back and never took part in the feast. I saw that with each backward movement of the Father's buttocks, by which the cord exited its sheath as far as the head, the lips of this part of Eradice's body opened up and appeared so brightly scarlet that he was delighted by the sight of it. I saw that, when the Father, by an opposite movement, pushed forward, these same lips, which could not be seen anymore for the black fur that covered them, tightened so exactly around his shaft, that it seemed swallowed up, that it would have been difficult to guess which of these two actors it belonged to, the kingpin appeared attached to the both of them.

What a mechanism! what clockwork! what a spectacle, my dear count, for a girl my age, who had no knowledge of this sort of mystery! What different ideas passed through my head, without being able to fix on any one of them! I remember only that I was twenty times on the verge of breaking out of that little room and throwing myself at the feet of that famous director of conscience, to beg him to treat me as he did my friend. Is this an act of concupiscence? That is what is still impossible for me to decide.

Let's get back to our actors. The Father's movements accelerated; he could barely keep his balance. His posture looked almost, from head to kneecaps, like the letter S, while his stomach came and went horizontally at Eradice's buttocks. It was this part of her body, which acted as a canal to his linchpin, which directed the action; and the two enormous eyesores that hung down between His Reverence's legs seemed like witnesses. "Your spirit is content, my little saint?" he let out with a sigh. "As for me, I see open skies; sufficient grace transports me; I..."

"Oh! Father," cried out Eradice, "what pleasure goads me! Yes, I enjoy celestial happiness; I feel my spirit is totally detached from matter: chase, my Father, chase all the rest of that impurity out of me. I see... the... an... gels; push deeper... push then... Ah!... oh!... good... St. Francis!... don't stop; I feel the cor... the cor... the cord... I can't go on... I'm dying!..."

The Father, who also felt the approach of sovereign pleasure, stammered, pushed, puffed, panted, and gasped. Finally, it was Eradice's last words that were the signal to him to beat a retreat: I saw the proud serpent become humble, grovelling, covered in scum as it exited its sheath.

All was put properly back in its place, and the Father, letting his robe fall, approached staggeringly the prie-dieu that Eradice had quit. There, feigning to enter into prayer, he ordered his penitent to get up, to cover herself, then to come and join him, to give thanks unto the Lord for the favors she had just received.

What else can I tell you, my dear count! Dirrag left her, and Eradice, who opened the door to the little room I was in, threw herself around my neck as she rushed at me. "Ah! my dear Thérèse," she said to me, "share in my happiness: yes, I saw paradise open up before me, I participated in the happiness of the angels. What pleasures, my friend, for a little moment of pain! By virtue of the holy cord, my soul nearly separated from matter. You were able to see where our good director inserted it into me. Well! I assure you that I felt it penetrate me as deep as my heart; one more inch of fervor and, no doubt about it, I'd have passed forever into the abode of the blessed."

Eradice detained me by a thousand other discourses in a tone of voice and with a liveliness of expression that left no doubt in my mind as to the reality of supreme happiness she had enjoyed. I was so moved that I could barely respond and congratulate her; extremely agitated, my heart pounding, I hugged her and left.

How many reflections I had then on the abuse that is done to the most respectable and established things in our society! With what artfulness this miserable bum leads his penitent to participate in his most shameless designs! He excites her imagination with the desire of becoming a saint; he persuades her that she will arrive there by detaching her spirit from the flesh. From there, he leads her by the necessity of undergoing a test of vigorous discipline: a ceremony that was doubtless a restorative for the hypocrite's enjoyment of pleasure, suitable to reviving the worn elasticity of his erectile nerve.[5] "You should feel nothing," he tells her, "see nothing, hear nothing, if your contemplation is perfect."

By those means, he is assured that she will not turn her head around, that she will see nothing of his shamelessness. The blows of the birch rods that he applies to her buttocks excite the spirits in that quarter he must attack, they heat them; and finally his recourse to the cord of St. Francis, prepared in advance, which, by its intromission, is supposed to chase out everything impure that remains in his penitent, lets him enjoy, without fear, the sexual favors of his docile proselyte; she believes that she falls into a purely spiritual and divine ecstasy, while she's actually enjoying the most sensuous pleasures of the flesh.

All of Europe had heard about the adventure of Father Dirrag and Mademoiselle Eradice, everyone discussed it and argued about it, but few people actually knew the backstory, which had devolved into a matter of taking sides between either the Monks or the Jesuits.[6] I won't repeat here what was said; you know everything that happened; you have seen the *factums*, the written documents that supported one side or the other, and you know what followed. Here

---

[5]erectile nerve: more exactly, the pelvic splanchnic nerves.

[6]Original footnote: the Monks or the Jesuits. In reality, this was a battle fought tooth and nail between the Jensenists and the Jesuits.

is the little I know about it, beyond what I just told you.

Mademoiselle Eradice is about my same age. She was born in Volnot, the daughter of a merchant, who provided lodging to my mother when she went to establish herself in that town. She had a fetching waist, and her skin was of exquisite beauty, ravishingly white; her hair was jet-black; with large, gorgeous eyes that had a virgin air to them. We were friends since childhood; but, when I was put in the convent, I lost contact with her. Her dominant passion was to distinguish herself among her companions, to make people talk about her. This passion, combined with a great fund of feelings, made her choose the path of devotion as most suitable to her designs. She loved God as one loves a lover. By the time I hooked up with her socially again, as Father Dirrag's penitent, her only conversation was on meditation, contemplation, and prayers; that was the fashion then followed by the mystical folks in town and in the province as well. Her modest manners had earned her a reputation for high virtue after a while. Eradice had spirit, but she applied it only to succeeding at satisfying the inordinate desire she had to make miracles; everything that stoked that passion became for her an incontestable truth. Weak humans are like this: the dominant passion they are affected by always subsumes all the others; they act only in consequence of that one passion; it prevents them from seeing the clearest and most obvious passion which should help destroy the other.

Father Dirrag was born in Lôde. At the time of

this adventure, he was about fifty-three years old; his face looked like what painters depict on satyrs. Although excessively ugly, he had something spiritual about his physiognomy. Bawdiness and impudicity were reflected in his eyes; in his actions, he seemed occupied only in the salvation of souls and for the glory of God. He had a lot of talent for the pulpit: his exhortations, his discourses, were full of sweetness and unction. He had the art of persuasion. Born with a tremendous amount of spirit, he employed it in acquiring the reputation for a spiritual *converter*; and, in fact, a considerable number of high-society women and girls resolved to practice penitence under his direction.

One can see that the similarity in character and views possessed by this Father and Mademoiselle Eradice sufficed to unite them. Also, from the very first moment he arrived in Volnot, where his reputation had already preceded him, Eradice threw herself, so to speak, into his arms. They had barely met when they both recognized in the other a means to augment their reciprocal glory. Eradice was certainly acting in good faith at the start; but Dirrag knew where to focus his attention: the lovely face of his new penitent seduced him, and he saw to it that he would seduce her in turn and would easily deceive her flexible, tender heart full of prejudices; her mind that accepted docilely every last drop of persuasion, and the ridiculousness of mystical insinuations and exhortations. It was then and there that he formed his plan of attack, as I have already described it above. The first step of that plan assured him of his sensuous amusement, of flogging, and for some time already the good Father had employed that same tactic with some of his other penitents: until then, it was where he drew the line in his libidinous pleasures with them; but the tightness, the contour, the whiteness of Eradice's buns had so heated and enflamed his imagination that he resolved to cross the line.

Great men break through the greatest of obstacles: this man imagined then the introduction of a portion of the cord of St. Francis, a relic, by whose intromission he might drive out all that remained impure and carnal within his penitent, and lead her to ecstasy. That's when he imagined the stigmata, in imitation of St. Francis' stigmata. He had one of his former penitents, who had his complete confidence, come secretly to Volnot and, with prior knowledge of his intentions, plant in Eradice's mind the ideas that he wanted her to possess. He found Eradice as yet too young and too enthusiastic in her desire to make miracles to risk entrusting her with his secret.

The former penitent arrived and soon became a religious friend of Eradice's, in whose mind she tried to insinuate a particular devotion for St. Francis, her patron. Father Dirrag and she concocted a special water that was supposed make wounds that looked like stigmata; and on Maundy Thursday, under the pretext of the Last Supper, the former penitent washed Eradice's feet and applied this water to them, which took its effect.

Two days later, Eradice confided in the old woman that she had a wound on each foot. "What happiness! What glory for you!" she exclaimed. "St. Francis has given you his stigmata. God wants to make you into a very great saint. Let's see if, like your great patron saint, your side would not also have the stigmata." She then placed her hand under the Eradice's left breast, where she again applied her special water: the following day, a new stigma.

Eradice couldn't help mentioning this miracle to her spiritual director, who, fearing a scandal, recommended that she practice humility and keep it under wraps. It was pointless; her dominant passion being the vanity to appear a saint, her joy could not be contained; she made confidences; her stigmata drew attention, and all the Father's penitents now wanted stigmata.

Dirrag felt it was necessary to support her reputation, but at the same time to try to make a diversion that would keep the public eye from remaining fixed on Eradice alone. Several other penitents were also therefore stigmatized by the same methods: his plan succeeded.

Meanwhile, Eradice devoted herself to St. Francis; her spiritual director assured her that he himself put the greatest trust in this saint's intercession; he added that he had effected a number of miracles by means of a large piece of this saint's cord, which a Jesuit Father had brought back for him from Rome, and that he had expelled, by virtue of this relic, the devil from several demoniacs' body, by introducing it into their mouth or some other natural orifice, depending on what was required. Finally, he showed her this fake cord, which was nothing other than a rather thick bit of cord, 8 inches in length, coated with mastic which made it hard and smooth. It was kept properly in a case lined with crimson velour, which acted like a kind of sheath; in short, it was one of those personal objects possessed by nuns and called a *dildo*. Clearly Dirrag had obtained this present from some old abbess, after insisting on it. Whatever the case, Eradice tried everything in the book to obtain permission to humbly kiss this relic, which the Father assured her could not be touched by profane hands without committing a crime.

This was how, my dear count, Father Dirrag gradually led his new penitent to suffer, over the course of several months, his shameless embraces, while she believed she was enjoying a purely spiritual and celestial happiness.

She's the one who told me all these details, some time after the judgment and trial. She confided in me that there was a certain monk (who had played an important role in this affair) who opened her eyes. He was young, handsome, well built, passionately in love with her, a friend of her father and mother, with whom he often ate together. He won her trust; he unmasked the shameless Dirrag; and I intuited clearly, through all that she told me, that she let herself be taken then in good faith by that lustful monk; I understood even that he had not gainsaid the reputation that his religious order possessed, and, by a happy conformation that included redoubled lessons, he compensated his new proselyte amply for the sacrifice that her old druid had exacted from her by that latter's weekly deceptions.

From the moment Eradice realized the dirty trick that had been played on her, i.e., Dirrag's having substituted the application of his loving member for the fake cord, the eloquence of the latter monk's demonstration made her feel grossly duped. Her vanity was wounded, and vengeance transported her to all the excesses that you know, in a concerted effort with her proud, newfound monk, who, over and above the bias that animated him, was still jealous of the favors Dirrag had sprung on his lover by surprise. Her charms were a property that, he believed, were created only for him to enjoy; it was an outright theft that had been committed, he claimed, and he professed to want to make an example of him; nothing short of roasting him, he contemplated, could satisfy his resentment and feelings of vengeance.

I have mentioned that, after Father Dirrag left Mademoiselle Eradice's room, I left too. As soon as I had returned to my room, I got down on my knees to beg God for the grace to be treated like my friend. My mind was in a highly agitated state that bordered on frenzy; an interior fire devoured me. One moment seated, the next moment standing, often on my knees, I could not stay still. I threw myself on the bed. I couldn't get it out of my head, the image of that rubicund member entering Eradice, without however attaching some distinct notion of pleasure, but still less of crime, to it. Finally I fell into a deep reverie in which it seemed to me that that same member, detached from any other object, made its entrance into *me* by the same route.

Unconsciously, I put myself into the same pose I had seen Eradice in, and unconsciously again, in my agitation, I slid back, while lying on my stomach, as far back as the column at the foot of the bed, which passed between my legs and thighs and stopped me from falling, and served as a point of fulcrum against that part of my body where I felt an inconceivable itch. The blow that it received by the column that stopped me caused me a little pain, which snapped me out of my revery, without diminishing the excess of my itching sensation. The position I found myself in required that I raise my backside in an attempt to free myself; this movement that I engaged in, of lifting and sliding my vagina up along the column, resulted in a friction that caused an extraordinary tickling sensation in me. I did it a second time, then a third, etc. which caused even more pleasure; suddenly I doubled-down with a kind of fury; without extricating myself, and with no other thought in my head, I began to move my buttocks with incredible agility, always gliding up and down the salutary column. Soon an overabundance of pleasure transported me, I lost consciousness, fainted, and fell into a deep sleep.

After two hours I woke again, my precious column still between my legs, lying on my stomach, my buns naked to the world. That posture surprised me; I remembered what had happened but only as one recalls a scene from a dream. However, feeling calmer now, the evacuation of that heavenly dew having left my mind freer, I reflected on everything I had witnessed in Eradice's room and on what had just happened in my own, without being able to draw any reasonable conclusion from any of it. The part of my body that had been rubbed up, and down, the column, as well as the upper inside portion of my thighs that had wrapped around it, made me feel seriously guilty; I dared consider it in my mind's eye, despite the prohibitions of my former director at the convent; but I hadn't dared touch myself with my hands: that had been too expressly forbidden.

As I was wrapping up this self-examination, my mother's servant came in to advise me that Madame C*** and M. the abbot T*** had arrived, that they were planning on staying for dinner, and that my mother was ordering me to come downstairs and keep them company; I did as I was told.

Quite some time had passed since I last saw Madame C***. Although she had shown much kindness to my mother, by her many services, and although she enjoyed the reputation of a very pious woman, her noticeable estrangement from Father Dirrag's maxims and mystical exhortations made me stop frequenting her, to avoid displeasing him: he was very strict on that score and didn't want his flock getting mixed up with those of other spiritual directors who were his competitors; doubtless he was afraid of people talking, and possible clarifications; in the end, it became a prerequisite condition, strongly recommended by His Reverence and very exactly observed by all those who comprised his flock.

However, there we were sitting down at the table together. The dinner was delightful. I felt much better than usual: my listlessness had given way to liveliness; no more pressure in the loins: on the contrary, I felt great. Unlike most meals with priests and religious devotees, we didn't speak ill of our neighbors. Abbot T***[7] who had lots of wit and even more experience, entertained us with a thousand little stories that had nothing to do with anyone's reputation and that brought joy to our hearts.

After having drunk some Champagne and taken her coffee, my mother pulled me aside and rebuked me sharply for the scant attention I had paid for some time now to Madame C***. "She's a lovely lady," she told me, "to whom I owe whatever consideration I enjoy in this town; her virtue, her knowledge, her wisdom have earned her the esteem and respect of all the people who know her; we need her support: I want you, and I command you, my daughter, to spend all your efforts engaged in preserving it." I responded to my mother that she had no reason to doubt my blind submission to her will. Alas! the poor woman had no idea of the nature of the lessons that I was about to receive from this lady, who enjoyed in fact the greatest of reputations.

My mother and I rejoined our guests. A few minutes later, I approached Madame C***, to whom I expressed apologies for my lack of propriety in paying her my respects; I implored her to allow me to repair the fault; I tried even to enter into some detail as to the reasons for this, but Madame C*** interrupted me without letting me finish. "I know," she said with kindness, "everything you are about to say: let's not enter into a discussion on subjects that are outside our competences; everyone has his reasons: perhaps they

---

[7]The Abbot Terray perhaps, the hero in *Ecclesiastical Laurels*, which Theresa was delighted to read; she says as much towards the end of this story. The *Ecclesiastical Laurels* is available in English translation by Sunny Lou Publishing.

are all good reasons; what is certain is that I will always receive you with great pleasure, and to begin to convince you of this," she added while raising her voice, "I would like to take you home with me this evening for supper. Is that okay?" she said to my mother. "On the condition that you and M. the abbot join us: right now you both have some business to attend to, so we will leave you to it. As for me, I will walk home with Mademoiselle Thérèse; you know the hour and the place of rendez-vous." My mother was delighted: Father Dirrag's maxims were not at all to her taste; she professed that Madame C***'s counsels would change my disposition away from quietism, which she suspected Father Dirrag to be practicing; perhaps even the two women were acting in concert. Whatever the case, they soon succeeded, beyond their expectations.

We left then, Madame C*** and I. But I had not taken one hundred steps when I felt a pain that became so strong I could barely remain standing. I made such horrible contortions. Madame C*** noticed. "What is it," she said, "my dear Thérèse? You look like you're in pain." Try as I might to convince her that it was nothing, women are naturally curious: she asked me a thousand questions which made me blush, the which didn't escape her. "You wouldn't happen to be," she said, "among the number of our famous stigmatized? Your feet can barely support you, and you are completely discountenanced. Come with me, my child, into the garden where you can get a hold of yourself." We were not far away. When we had entered the garden, we sat down in a charming little shelter that looked out onto the sea.

After some vague conversation, Madame C*** asked me again point-blank whether I had stigmata and how was I finding Father Dirrag's spiritual guidance. "I can't hide from you," she added, "that I am so surprised by this kind of miracle that I ardently desire to see it for myself if it really exists: come on, my dear little friend," she continued, "open up to me: tell me everything you know; explain to me in what way and when these wounds appeared; you can be assured that I will keep everything you say in the strictest confidence, and I think you know me well enough not to doubt it."

If women are curious, women also love to talk: I have this last fault myself; besides, several glasses of Champagne had gone to my head: I was in a lot of pain; it didn't take much to make me spill the beans. I responded at first totally naturally to Madame C*** that I had the good fortune of being among our Lord's elect, but that this very morning I had seen Mademoiselle Eradice's stigmata, and that the Very Reverend Father Dirrag had visited her in my presence. New overzealous questions on the part of Madame C***, who imperceptibly pressured me into giving her an account, in minutest detail, leaving nothing out, not only what I had seen in Eradice's room, but also what had happened to me in my room, and the pains that resulted from it.

During the course of this most unusual recitation, Madame C*** was prudent enough not to betray the least surprise: she praised all in order to entice me to tell all. When I found myself struggling to find the words to explain the ideas behind what I had seen, she exacted from me descriptions of lasciviousness that must have greatly pleased her coming from the mouth of a girl my age and also so simple a one as myself. Never perhaps have so many infamies been said and heard with so much gravity.

When I had finished speaking, Madame C*** seemed sunk in deep thought; she responded only by monosyllables to the questions I put forward. Having gotten a hold of herself, she told me that everything she had just heard had something quite singular to it, and warranted great attention; that while I was waiting for her to tell me what she thought and what course she recommended I take, before anything else I needed to attend to the pain I was feeling, soaking in warm wine the parts of my body that had been bruised by rubbing them up against the column of my bed. "Be careful," she told me, "my dear child, to mention nothing of what you've just confided in me to your mother, nor to anyone else, much less to Father Dirrag. There's both good and bad in all this. Come and visit me again tomorrow at around nine o'-clock in the morning, I'll tell you more; you can count on my friendship: the excellence of your heart and character have earned you that much. I see your mother advancing now; let's go meet her and talk about other things now."

M. abbot T*** arrived a quarter of an hour later. One sups early in the country; it was then seven thirty in the evening; supper was served and we sat down at the table.

During supper, Madame C*** could not help letting escape several satirical swipes at Father

Dirrag; the abbot appeared surprised by this, and he found fault with her delicately. “Why,” he continued, “do we not let others follow the conduct they think is best for them, so long as they do not violate the established order? So far, we see nothing in Father Dirrag that does not conform; permit me, Madame, to not share your opinion, until the events justify the ideas that you want me to have of this Father.” Madame C***, to avoid having to respond, adroitly changed subject. They got up from the table at ten o’clock; Madame C*** whispered a few words into the ear of M. the abbot, who was exiting with my mother and me and accompanied us home.

As it is right, my dear count, that you should know just what this Madame C*** and M. the abbot T*** are all about, I think it is time that I give you an idea.

Madame C*** was born a young lady. Her parents constrained her to wed at fifteen years old an old naval officer who was sixty years old. This latter man died five years into the marriage and left Madame C*** pregnant with a son who, on entering the world, nearly caused his mother’s death in childbirth. This child died three months later, and Madame C*** found herself, with this death, the inheritress of a considerably large fortune. Widow, pretty, independent at the age of twenty, her hand in marriage was soon pursued by all eligible bachelors in the province; but she was so outspoken as to her plans never to put herself in harms way again, the dangers of which she had miraculously escaped, that even the most assiduous suitors soon abandoned the idea.

Madame C*** was very witty; she had strong feelings, which she adopted only after thorough inspection. She read much and loved to converse on the most abstract subjects. Her conduct was without reproach. An essential friend, she gave assistance when she could. My mother could attest to that. She was twenty-six years old then; I will have the opportunity, later on, of describing her face to you.

M. the abbot T***, a special friend of Madame C***'s and also her director of conscience, was a man of true merit. He was forty-four or forty-five years old: short, but well proportioned, with an open physiognomy, spiritual, a careful observer of the decorum inherent in his position, well-loved and sought after by influential people, whom he delighted. To a witty mind he added extensive knowledge. His good qualities, widely recognized, had allowed him to obtain the position he held, and I should stop there. He was the confessor and friend of people of substance of both sexes, just as Father Dirrag was the confessor of religious devotees by profession, enthusiasts, quietists, and fanatics.

I returned the following day to Madame C***'s house, at the hour agreed on. "Well! my dear Thérèse," she said to me as I entered, "how goes it with the afflicted parts? Did you sleep well?"

"Everything's better, madame," I said to her; "I did what you prescribed. Everything's been well soaked, that helped a great deal; but I hope at least I've not offended God." Madame C*** smiled, and after having had me served with a cup of coffee, she said, "What you confided in me yesterday," she said to me, "is more serious than you think. I thought it necessary to speak with M. T***. about it, who's waiting for you now at the confessional. I insist that you go find him and repeat to him word for word everything you told me. He's an honest man and has good advice: you need it. I think he'll prescribe for you a new way of conducting yourself, which is necessary for your health and for your salvation. Your mother would die of grief if she knew what I know; for I cannot hide from you that what you saw in Mademoiselle Eradice's room are dreadful things. Go then, Thérèse, go and give a full report to M. T***: you won't regret it."

I burst into tears, and I left her house trembling all over as I went to seek out M. T***, who entered his confessional as soon as he saw me.

I concealed nothing from M. T***, who listened to me attentively until I had finished, and interrupted me only to ask for certain explanations about things he didn't understand. "You have come," he said, "to tell me some very astonishing things: Father Dirrag is a false-hearted, miserable rogue, who has let himself be carried away by his sexual passion; he marches straight to his damnation and brings Mademoiselle Eradice with him; be that as it may, mademoiselle, we must pity them rather than blame them. We are not always in a position to resist temptation; the happiness and unhappiness of our lives is often a consequence of these sorts of occasion. Do what you can to avoid them then; stop seeing Father Dirrag and all his penitents, without speaking ill of any of them: charity would ask as much. Frequent Madame C***;

she has taken a liking to you, and she will give you good counsel and a good example to follow."

"Let us talk now, my child, of those excessive 'tickling' feelings in that part of your body that you rubbed up against the column of your bed; those are sexual desires, as natural as hunger and thirst: you must not seek them out nor excite them; but as soon as you feel a strong urge, there is nothing wrong with taking your hand, your finger, and rubbing that part of your body until you are satisfied, as needed. I expressly forbid you however from inserting your finger into the opening you find there; for now, just know that it could work against you in the mind of your future husband. That said, given this is, I repeat, a need excited in us by the immutable laws of nature, our hands, also from nature, give us the remedy to satisfy that need, as I have indicated to you.

"Now, as we are assured that natural law is a divine institution, how could we fear to offend God by relieving our needs by the means he has given to us, who are his work, especially when these means cause no harm to the established order of society? It is not the same, my dear girl, as with what has transpired between Father Dirrag and Mademoiselle Eradice: this Father has deceived his penitent, he risks impregnating her by replacing the pretended cord of St. Francis with his natural male member, which serves to procreate. In so doing, he has sinned against natural law, which prescribes that we love our neighbor as ourselves. Is this loving one's neighbor by putting, as he has done, Mademoiselle Eradice in danger of losing her reputation and dishonoring her for life?

"The insertion, my dear child, of this Father's member, and the actions you have seen performed by it, in and around the natural part of his penitent's body, which is the mechanism by which babies are produced, is forbidden outside the state of marriage: when performed on a girl, this action can harm the tranquility of families and disturb public interest, which must always be respected. Thus, while you are as yet unmarried, be careful not to allow any man to perform like operation on you, in any way, shape or form whatsoever. I have indicated to you a remedy that will moderate the excess of your desires and temper the fire that excites them. This same remedy will contribute in no time to re-establishing your faltering health and help you to regain some weight. Your cute face will not fail to attract suitors who seek to seduce you. Be on your guard then and never forget the lessons I am giving you now. That is all for today, child," added this sensible-minded spiritual director. "You will find me here in one week, at the same time; if nothing else, remember that everything that is said in the Sacrament of Penance must be as sacred for the penitent as for the confessor, and that it is an enormous sin to reveal the least circumstance of it to anyone."

My new director's precepts charmed my soul; I saw in them a strong demonstration of reason, a principle of charity that made me feel the ridiculousness of what I had heard up until that time.

After having passed the remainder of the day in reflection, in the evening, before going to bed, I prepared to soak my bruised nether parts: at ease before the eyes of God insofar as fondling myself was concerned, I lifted my nightshirt; and as I sat on the edge of my bed, my legs spread apart as best I could, and set about examining attentively that part of my body that makes me a woman, I opened the lips partway and felt around with my finger for the opening through which Father Dirrag had been able to insert his fat instrument into Eradice; I discovered it, but was unable to persuade myself that I had found it: its smallness made me unsure of myself, and I attempted to introduce my finger into it when I remembered what M. T*** had said: I pulled it out promptly. A small protuberance that I encountered caused me to shiver; I held my hand there, I rubbed it, and soon I arrived at the climax of pleasure. What a happy discovery for a girl who had within herself an abundant store of the essence that is life's principle!

I wallowed for six months in a torrential stream of sensual pleasure, without anything of importance to write about here.

My health was entirely restored; my conscience was clean, because of the attentions of my new spiritual director, who gave me wise counsel combined with human feelings of passion: I saw him regularly every Monday, in the confessional, and every day at Madame C***'s house. I was inseparable from this kind woman: the dark clouds in my mind had dissipated; consequently, little by little I grew accustomed to thinking, to reasoning. No more Father Dirrag or Eradice for me.

How an example and the precepts are such

great teachers for instructing hearts and minds! If it was true that they were not helpful and that each person had within himself the seeds of what he is capable of, what is certain at least is that they serve to develop those seeds and make us perceive the ideas and feelings we are susceptible to, and that, without example, without lessons, those seeds would remain buried under their obstacles and in their hard outer casings.

Meanwhile, my mother continued to run her wholesale business, which was doing poorly; customers owed her lots of money, and she was on the verge of going bankrupt because of one merchant in Paris, who was capable of ruining her. After some deliberation, she decided to make a trip to that superb city. This tender mother of mine loved me too much to want to lose sight of me during her absence, which could have been quite long; it was resolved that I would accompany her. Alas! the poor woman could hardly have known that she would finish her sad days there and that I would find, in the arms of my dear count, the source of all my happiness in life.

It was decided that we would leave in one month, after I had spent some time with Madame C***, at her house in the country, at a distance of one league from town. M. the abbot T*** visited regularly, every day, and spent the night there when his responsibilities permitted. Each one of them smothered me in caresses; they no longer hesitated to speak freely in front of me, about matters of morality, religion, metaphysics, in a manner quite different from how I had received these same principles. I apperceived that Madame C*** was content with my way of thinking and reasoning, and that she took pleasure in leading me, from minor to major premise, to clear and evident proofs. Only sometimes I was aggrieved to discover the abbot T*** making a sign to her to lay off pursuing her reasonings any further on certain matters. This discovery humiliated me; I resolved to do everything I could to be instructed in the principles he wanted to hide from me. Until then, I hadn't the least suspicion of the mutual feelings of affection that existed between them.

You will see, my dear count, the well from which I drew the principles of morality and metaphysics that you have so well cultivated in me and which, by clarifying to me who we are in this world as well as what we have to fear from one another, guarantees the tranquility in a life that you take so much pleasure in.

We spent the most beautiful days of summer there; Madame C*** rose ordinarily at five o'clock in the morning to take a walk in the grove at the back of her garden. I had noticed that the abbot T*** joined her as well when he spent the night in the country, and that after an hour or two they returned together to Madame C***'s bedroom; neither of them showed their face in the house until about eight or nine o'clock in the morning.

I resolved to anticipate them in the grove and hide myself in such a way that I could hear them. Because I hadn't the shadow of a suspicion of their love for each other, I had no idea what I was missing by not *seeing* them. So I reconnoitered the terrain and assured myself of a spot suitable to my designs.

In the evening, while we supped, the conversation turned to the operations and productions of nature. "But what is this nature, then?" asked Madame C***. "Is it something particular? Isn't everything produced by God? Would it be a subaltern divinity?"

"In truth, you are acting unreasonably by speaking about it like this," replied M. the abbot T***, while winking at her. "I promise you," he said, "in our walk, tomorrow morning, to explain to you the idea one ought to have of this common mother of the human species: it is too late now to touch on the matter. Don't you see that it would bore Mademoiselle Thérèse to tears, who is already nodding off in her chair? What do you say we all call it a night; I need to finish my prayers,[8] and I will follow your example shortly thereafter." M. the abbot's suggestion was accepted; everyone retired to his room.

The following day, at the break of dawn, I went to lie in wait. I hid in the bushes that were behind a kind of wooded arbor, provisioned with wooden benches, painted green, and some statues. After an hour of impatience, I heard my heroes arrive and sit down precisely on the bench behind which I was crouching.

"Yes, in truth," said the abbot on entering the bower, "she grows prettier every day; her tits have grown large enough to fill the hand of an honest ecclesiastic; her eyes have a liveliness to them that no-

[8]finish my prayers: given the time of day, these are most likely the compline. There were (are) seven traditional canonical hours of the day: lauds, prime, terce, sext, none, vespers, and compline, not to mention the night office of matins.

wise contradicts the fire of her sexual desire, for she has one of the strongest, that little saucy Thérèse. Can you imagine that by taking advantage of the permission I gave her to relieve herself with her finger, she does it at least once a day. You have to admit that I am also a good doctor and docile confessor; I have healed her, in both body and spirit."

"But, abbot," responded Madame C***, "will you soon stop talking about Thérèse? Have we come here to converse only about her beautiful eyes and her strong sexual desire? I suspect, my dirty-minded sir, that you would like nothing better than to help her relieve her suffering. For all that, you know I'm a good sport, and I'd consent willingly if I didn't see any danger in it for you. Thérèse is a clever girl; but she's too young and hasn't enough experience in the world for you to risk confiding in her. I notice that her curiosity is unparalleled. She's got the potential to become a very good subject; and if it weren't for the drawbacks I just mentioned, I'd be all for proposing a *ménage à trois* with her; for let's admit it – it's quite crazy to be jealous or envious of the happiness of one's friends so long as their felicity subtracts nothing from our own."

"You are quite right, madame," said the abbot: "those are two passions that torment, to no avail, all those who were not born to know how to think. One must distinguish however envy from jealousy. Envy is a passion innate in man; it is part of his essence: children in the cradle are envious of what is given to other children. Education alone can moderate the effects of this passion that one has received by the hand of nature. But it is different with jealousy, with respect to sexual desire. This passion is the result of our self-esteem and prejudice. We are aware of entire nations where men offer the pleasure of their wives to their guests, just as we offer the best wine in our cellar to ours. In one of these nations of islanders, the husband caresses the lover while he is enjoying the embraces of his wife; his compatriots applaud him, and congratulate him. A Frenchman, in the same situation, pulls a long face: everyone points at him and mocks him. A Persian stabs his lover and his mistress to death: everyone applauds his double assassination.

"It is evident then that jealousy is not something we get from nature: it comes from education, from the prejudice of a people. From childhood, a girl, in Paris, reads and hears it said that it is humiliating to suffer an infidelity by one's lover; one assures a young man that a mistress, that an unfaithful woman, wounds his self-esteem, dishonors the lover or the friend. It is from these principles, suckled as it were from our mother's breasts, that jealousy is born, this monster that torments humans to no avail, for a wrong that does not even exist.

"But let us examine the inconstancy of infidelity for a moment. I love a woman who loves me back: our characters are well suited to one another; her face, my pleasure in her, her enjoyment of me, all make me happy; then she leaves me: now, the pain I feel is no longer the result of prejudice, – it is rational. I have lost something tangible, a habitual source of pleasure, which I am not certain I can get back again with all its agreeableness; but a *passing* infidelity that is due to nothing more than pleasure, sexual desire, sometimes gratefulness, a tender feeling, or for someone else's pleasure, – what harm is there in this? To be honest, say what you will, a person must be out of his mind to get all worked up over what is rightly referred to as *much ado about nothing*, about something that is intrinsically neither good nor bad."

"Oh! I see where you're going with this," said Madame C***, interrupting the abbot T***; "what you're telling me, quite sweetly, is that by the goodness of your heart, or to make Thérèse happy, you'd be all for giving her a little lesson in the pleasures of the flesh, a friendly little squirt in the ass that, in your opinion, shouldn't affect me one way or the other. My dear abbot," she continued, "I consent with all my heart: I love the both of you; you'd both benefit from this test, and I'd lose nothing by it. Why should I oppose it? If I got upset, you'd conclude with good reason that I'm interested only in myself, in my own private satisfaction, in augmenting it at the expense of what you could enjoy elsewhere anyways; but that's simply not the case: I know how to make myself happy independently of anything that might contribute to the increase of your own pleasure. And so, my dear friend, without fear of offending me, go ahead and ride, ride Thérèse's bush as you see best; knock yourself out; it'll do that poor little girl a world of good; but I repeat: don't be imprudent..."

"What madness!" rejoined the abbot, "I swear to you I am not thinking of Thérèse at all. I merely wanted to explain to you the mechanism by which nature..."

"Oh boy! let's drop it," replied Madame C***. "But, as for *nature*, you forget, it seems to me, the promise you made me to define just what you mean by this good mother of ours. Let's see how you get yourself out of this demonstration, given you claim you can demonstrate anything."

"You want me to?" responded the abbot; "but, my little woman, you know what must be done first; I lack motivation when I have not engaged in the act that most actively affects my imagination. My other thoughts are unclear and always subsumed, confounded by this one. I have told you before, in Paris when I was dedicated exclusively to my studies and the most abstract sciences, the moment I felt the urge of the flesh goad me on, I had a young girl *ad hoc*, like someone picks up a chamberpot to piss in, with whom I satisfied my great need one or two times, in a way you are disinclined to. At which time, my mind quieted, my thoughts cleared, I resumed my work, and I maintain that every man of letters, every bureaucrat who possesses a small sexual desire, ought to practice this remedy, as necessary to the health of the body as to that of the mind. I will go even further: I put forward that every honest man familiar with the obligations he has to society ought to do likewise, to avoid getting himself so horny that he forgets his obligations and debauches the first wife or daughter of his friends or neighbors who comes along.

"Now, you will ask me, maybe, madame," continued the abbot, "how should girls and boys behave? They have, you say, their needs like grownups do; they are made of the same clay; however they cannot take advantage of the same resources: their honor, their fear of an indiscretion, a blunder, or of making children, does not allow them to have recourse to the same remedies as grownups. Besides, you will add, where will you find such men all ready to go, as my little girl was, *ad hoc*?

"Well! madame," continued the abbot T***, "women and girls should do like Thérèse and you do; if that game does not satisfy them enough (as in fact it does not satisfy everyone), they should make use of those ingenious instruments called *dildos*; they are a rather natural imitation of reality. Add to this that one can make use of her imagination. At the end of the day, I repeat, men and women ought to procure for themselves the pleasures that do not trouble the foundations of established society. Women, then, must enjoy only what is proper for them, keeping in mind the duties imposed on them by the establishment. You may cry injustice all you want; what you consider to be a personal injustice ensures society's general well-being, which nobody should attempt to infringe on."

"Oh! I get it, mister abbot sir," replied Madame C***; "you've just now informed me that a woman, a girl, mustn't do as men do, which you know a lot about, and that an honest man mustn't disturb public interest by seeking to seduce them, while you yourself, M. Rakehell himself, you've tormented me a hundred times to submit to that very thing, and which long ago would've been a done deal if it weren't for the insurmountable fear I've always had of becoming pregnant; you've not been afraid then, while satisfying yourself, of acting against the general interests that you extol so highly."

"Here we go again," responded the abbot. "Are you going to start singing that song again, my dear woman? Have I not told you that by taking certain precautions you run no risk of that inconvenience? Have you not agreed with me that women have but three things to fear: the devil, their reputation, and getting pregnant? You are quite at ease, I think, on the first article; as for the second, I have no reason to believe that you are afraid of an indiscretion or an imprudence from me, which alone could tarnish your reputation; finally, one becomes a mother only by the thoughtlessness of her lover. Now, I have already proven to you, more than once, by explanation of the mechanism by which babies are made, that there is nothing easier to avoid; let us go over again what I have said on this subject.

"The lover, at the thought, or on sight, of his mistress, finds himself in a state necessarily conducive to the act of generation: the blood, the spirits, his erectile nerves, have swollen and hardened his prick; with both parties in agreement, they get into position; the lover's arrow is pushed into his mistress's quiver; the seeds get ready through the reciprocal rubbing of their parts. The excess of pleasure transports them; already the divine elixir is ready to flow; then, the wise lover, master of his passions, removes the bird from its nest, and his hand, or his mistress's hand, succeeds in achieving, by some light movements, ejaculation *on the outside*. No children to fear in this case. The thoughtless and brutish lover, on the contrary, pushes deep into the vagina: he scatters his seed there; it penetrates the womb, and from there into her Fallopian tubes, where the egg is inseminated.

"There you have it, madame," continued Monsieur T***, "because you wanted me to repeat it again, that is the mechanism by which babies are made. Knowing me as you do, can you believe me to be among the latter group of imprudent men? No, my dear friend, I have one hundred times the experience to the contrary. Let me, I beg you, propose it to you again today; look at what a state of triumph my funny little man is in: you hold it. – Yes! – Squeeze it in your hand; as you can see it is begging for mercy, and I..."

"Do not, *please*, my dear abbot," replied at this moment Madame C***. "You're just wasting your breath, I'm telling you; nothing that you've said to me just now can calm my fears, and I'd procure for you a pleasure that I couldn't enjoy myself: that's not right. Let me do it this way then; I'll instill some reason into this little shameless fellow. Ah, well!" she continued, "are you satisfied with my tits and thighs? Have you kissed them and handled them enough? Why're you rolling my sleeves up like that above the elbows? You, sir, no doubt love to see the movement of a naked arm. Am I doing it right? You're not saying anything! Ah! the naughty little scamp! Look how happy he is!"

A moment of silence ensued. Then suddenly I heard the abbot exclaim: "My dear woman, I cannot take it any more: a little faster; give me a little tongue then, I beg you. Oh! it co...mes!"

Imagine for yourself, my dear count, the state of agitation I was in during this edifying conversation. I tried twenty times to rise in order to find some opening in the bushes by which to see, but the noise of the leaves kept holding me back always. I was seated; I stretched myself out as best I could; and to put out the fire that was devouring me, I resorted to my ordinary little practice.

After several moments, which were employed doubtless in cleaning up after M. the abbot: "To tell you the truth," he said, "when all is said and done, I believe, my good friend, that you were right to refuse me the enjoyment I was asking of you: I felt such a vivid pleasure, such a powerful stimulation, that I think I would have made an awful mistake, if you had let me proceed.

"It must be admitted that we are quite feeble animals and poor masters of our will," he added.

"I know all about that, my poor abbot," resumed Madame C***; "you've taught me nothing new; but tell me, in the kinds of activity we take pleasure in, are we not sinning against the interests of society? And that wise lover whose prudence you make so much of, who takes the bird out of its nest and scatters the balm of life on the outside, doesn't he perform a crime as well? For you must agree that we, the two of us, remove from society a citizen that could become useful to it."

"My reasoning," replied the abbot, "appears specious at first, but you will see, my beautiful lady, it is merely the rough exterior. We have no human nor divine law that invites us, still less one that constrains us, to work towards the multiplication of the species. All these laws allow for celibacy among boys and girls, and among a swarm of useless religious and lazy monks; they permit a married man to possess his pregnant wife, even though the seed scattered at that time is not expected to come to fruition. Virginity even is reputed preferable to marriage.

"Now, with these facts put forward, is it not certain that the man who cheats on his wife and the people, like us, who enjoy innocent little pleasures, do no differently than those monks, and those religious, and everyone else who lives in celibacy? The latter conserve in their loins fruitlessly the seed that the former scatter fruitlessly: are they not therefore, one and all, precisely in the same situation, as far as society is concerned? Neither one of them brings a citizen into society; but does not sound reason dictate to us that it is better to enjoy a pleasure that harms no one, by spreading that seed without utility, than to keep it in our seminal vesicles not only with the same inutility, but worse still – at the expense of our health and often our life. So you see, Madame Quibbler," added the abbot, "that our pleasures cause no more damage to society than the approved celibacy of monks, and religious, etc.; and that we can continue doing as we have done all along."

It was clear that, subsequent to these reflections, the abbot was about to render Madame C*** a service, because I heard, a moment later, her saying to him: "Ah! stop, you naughty abbot, remove your finger; I don't want to today, I'm still recovering from our follies from yesterday; let's put this off until tomorrow; besides, you know that I like to be at my ease, by which I mean lying on my bed: this bench is not comfortable; stop, I said, – the only thing I want from you right now is that definition you promised me about Lady Nature; there, you've become calm again, Mister Philosopher; speak, and I'll listen."

"On Lady Nature?" responded the abbot, "My faith! you know as much about her as I do. She is an imaginary being, it is a word devoid of meaning. The first leaders of religion, the first politicians, finding themselves in a bind because of the idea they had to give to the public of moral good and evil, imagined a being between God and us, which they made the author of our passions, our illnesses, our crimes. How, in fact, without this aid, would they have reconciled their system with God's infinite kindness? Where would those desires to steal, lie, rape, kill have come from, which they told us about? Why so many illnesses and weaknesses? What had that unfortunate legless cripple done to God, who was born to crawl on the ground his entire life?

"A theologian tells us this: '*Those are the effects of nature.*' But, what is that nature he refers to? Is it another God that we do not know about? Does it act on its own, independently of God's will? 'No,' the theologian tells us again dryly. 'Given God cannot be the author of evil, evil can only exist by means of nature.' What absurdity! Is it the stick that hits me that I should complain about? Is it not the man who directed the blow? Is he not the author of the evil I feel?

"Why not agree, once and for all, that nature

is a figment of our imagination, a word devoid of meaning; that everything comes from God; that a physical malady that harms some people provides happiness to others; that all is good; that there is no evil in the world as far as Divinity is concerned; that everything labeled morally *good* or *evil* is relative to the interests of societies established by men, but also relative to God by the will with which we act, by necessity, according to the first principles set in motion, that he established in everything that exists? A man steals, he does good as far as he is concerned; he does evil, by his infraction of the established rules of society, but it has nothing to do with God. However, I agree that this man must be punished, even if he acted by necessity, even if I am convinced that he had no choice whether to commit his crime or not; but he must be punished, because the punishment of a man who disturbs the established order makes automatically, by means of the senses, impressions on the soul that prevent naughty people from risking something that would bring down on them the same punishment, and that the pain this wretch feels for his infraction should contribute to the general happiness, which is preferable in this case to a private good.

"I might even add that one cannot overemphasize the infamy also of parents, friends, and all those who have regular relations with a criminal, in order to involve, by this political connection, all humans, so that they might be mutually inspired as a group by the horror of actions and crimes that disturb the public peace, a peace that our natural disposition, our private needs, and our personal well-being lead us unfailingly to infringe; a disposition, finally, that cannot be instilled in a man except by education, by means of impressions he receives in the soul through contact with other human beings he frequents or sees regularly, by their good example, or by their discourse; in a word, by external sensations that, joined together with internal dispositions, regulate all our life's actions. One must goad then, one must by necessity excite, men collectively by these sensations that are useful to overall happiness.

"I think, madame," added the abbot, "that you now know what one means by the word *nature*. I propose to discuss with you tomorrow morning the idea that one ought to have of religion. It is a topic important for our happiness; but it is too late this morning to dig into it. I feel I need to go have my chocolate."

"That's fine," said Madame C***, standing up. "M. the Philosopher doubtless has need of a physical reparation, for the libidinous outflows I caused him; it's only right," she continued; "for you've done and said admirable things: there's nothing better than your observations on nature; don't take it amiss if I say that I highly doubt you can make me see as clearly on the topic of religion, which you've tried on multiple occasions with much less success. How to give, in effect, demonstrations on so abstract a subject matter and where everything's an article of faith?"

"That is what you will find out tomorrow," replied the abbot.

"Oh! I don't plan on letting you get off the hook today by your excuses," rejoined Madame C***: "let's go back now, if you don't mind, to my room, where I've need of you and my couch."

Several instants later, they walked together down the path back to the house; I followed them by a covered lane. I stayed in my room only long enough to change my dress, and I went to Madame C***'s rooms where I was afraid the abbot had already begun his discussion on religions, which I absolutely had to hear. His discourse on nature had knocked me for a loop: I saw clearly that God and nature acted only through the immediate will of God. From there I drew my own small inferences, and I began perhaps to think for the very first time in my life.

I trembled on entering Madame C***'s rooms; it seemed to me she was bound to have detected my perfidy from earlier and the divers reflections that stirred within me. The abbot T*** looked at me attentively: I thought I was ruined; but soon I heard him talking in a low voice to Madame C***: "Look at Thérèse and how pretty she is! Her colors are charming; her eyes penetrating, and her physiognomy becomes more spiritual by the day." I don't know what Madame C*** said to him in response; they both smiled. I pretended not to have seen, and I made a great effort to stay close to them all day.

Returning to my room that evening, I formulated my plan for the following morning. The fear that I had of not waking early enough was the reason for my not sleeping at all that night. Toward five o'clock in the morning, I saw Madame C*** approaching the grove, where Monsieur T*** was already waiting for her. According to what I had heard the day before, she was going to return soon to her bedroom, where the couch was located that she had mentioned. I didn't hesitate to rush to her room and hide on the other side of her bed, where I sat down on the floor, my back against the wall, next to the bedhead. The bed curtain was in front of me; I could open it a crack if need be to have before my eyes the entire spectacle on the couch, which was at the opposite corner of the room, where they could not say a word without my hearing it.

Thus positioned, impatience began to make me fear I had missed my opportunity, when suddenly the two actors returned. "Lay me properly, my dear friend," said Madame C***, lying back on her couch. "Reading that nasty book, *The Story of the Charterhouse Porter,* has made me horny; his portraits are striking; they've an air of truth about them that's charming; if it was less smutty, it'd be an inimitable book of that genre. Put it inside me today, abbot, I beg you," she added; "I'm dying of desire, and I'm willing to take the risk."

"Not me," replied the abbot, "for two good reasons: first, because I love you, and I am too honest of a man to risk your reputation and your just reproaches for such an imprudence; second, because M. the doctor is not today, as you can see, so very brilliant; I am not a Gascon, and..."

"I can see for myself," replied Madame C***; "your second reason is so convincing that you could've, honestly, dispensed with the first. Lie down next to me then," she added extending herself lasciviously on the couch, "and recite, as you call it, the *Lit-*

tle Office."[9]

"Ah! with all my heart, my dear woman," replied the abbot T***, who was still standing, as he uncovered Madame C***'s breasts methodically. Next he lifted her dress and her shirt above the navel, while he spread her thighs and raised her knees up a bit, in such a way that her heels, brought close to her buttocks, pressed against a leg of the couch, each to each.

In this position, partially hidden from me by the abbot, who was kissing, successively, one part of her body after the other, his dear mistress, Madame C*** remained motionless, contemplative, meditating on the nature of pleasure, the first fruits of which she was already starting to enjoy. Her eyes were half-closed, the tip of her tongue could be seen at the edge of her vermillion lips, and all the muscles in her face were in a state of sensuous agitation. "Enough with the kisses already," she said to the abbot T***; "don't you see that I'm waiting for you? I can't wait any longer."

The complaisant director of conscience never made her repeat her request twice. He slid onto the foot of the couch between Madame C*** and the wall, his left hand was passed under her head, and he squeezed her, kissing her on the mouth with small, extremely voluptuous movements of his tongue. His other hand was busy with the main action: it caressed her artistically, rubbing that part of the her body that distinguishes our sex, and which is abundantly gar-

[9]The Little Office: *The Little Office of the Blessed Virgin Mary.*

nished on Madame C***'s body with a full patch of the most beautifully black curly hair.

Never before has a scene been put in a more advantageous light, from where I sat. The couch was positioned such that Madame C***'s bush was in full view. Beneath her I saw a portion of her buttocks, gently agitated by a movement that went from low to high, which announced the internal fermentation she was experiencing, and the most beautiful, round, and white thighs ever imaginable made another small movement together with her knees, from right to left and back again, whose swaying contributed also clearly to the joy she felt in the principal part of her body which was being feted, and whose movements the abbot's finger, lost in her fleece, followed.

It would be pointless for me to try to tell you, my dear count, what I was thinking at that moment: I felt nothing because I felt too much. Unconsciously, I aped what I was seeing; my hand imitated that of the abbot's; I copied all my friend's movements. "Oh! I'm dying!" she cried out suddenly; "put it in, my dear abbot; yes!... higher... I implore you; use all your strength and push, my dear... Ah! what pleasure!... I melt!... I... am... swoo... ning...!"

Always the perfect imitator of what I saw, without reflecting for an instant on what my director had forbidden me to do, I buried my finger in turn; I felt a certain pain, but it didn't stop me, and I reached orgasm.

Flights of sensuality were followed by incredible feelings of euphoria, and I had nearly fallen asleep in spite of my uncomfortable situation when I heard Madame C*** approaching where I was hidden: I thought the game was up, but I got off easy in spite of my fear. She pulled the cord that rang the bell and asked for chocolate, which they nibbled on while making apologies for the pleasures they had just enjoyed. "Why aren't they entirely innocent?" Madame C*** lamented, "you've spoken so eloquently about their not harming any of society's interests, that we're moved by a need that's quite natural to certain temperaments, as necessary to quench as hunger or thirst; you've quite well demonstrated that we act only by God's will, and that nature's a word empty of meaning of which God is merely the cause; but what about religion? Religion forbids us the pleasures of sex outside of matrimony. Is that a word lacking in meaning too?"

"What! madame," rejoined the abbot, "have you forgotten that we are not at all free to decide for ourselves? How can we sin? But let us dig deeper into the matter of religion if you want to. Your discretion, your prudence are well known to me, and I have less fear explaining myself to you than protesting before God of the good faith with which I have sought to untangle illusion's truth. Here is a quick summary of my labors and reflections on this important topic:

"God is good, I say; his goodness assures me that if I seek with ardor to understand if it is a veritable worship that he demands of me, he will not trick me; evidently I will come to know this worship, otherwise God would be unjust; he gave me reason employ, to guide me: how better to use it?

"If a Christian of good faith does not want to examine his religion, why would he want (as he demands) a Mohammedan of good faith to examine his own? They believe, each of them, that their religion has been revealed to them by God, the one by Jesus Christ, the other by Mohammed.

"We arrive at faith only because men have told us that God has revealed certain truths. But other men have said the same thing to sectarians of other religions; who to believe? In order to find out, one must examine them, because everything that comes from men must be subjected to our reason.

"All the authors of divers religions across the globe have vaunted that God had revealed their religions to them; who to believe? Let us examine which one is the true one; but as everything is prejudiced from our childhood and by our education, to judge soundly, one must begin by making a sacrifice of all our prejudices before God and examining then, with the light of reason, a thing on which our happiness or unhappiness depends, throughout our life and for all eternity.

"I observe to begin with that the world is divided into four parts; that the twentieth portion, at most, of one of these four parts is Catholic; that all the inhabitants of the other parts claim that we adore a man and bread; that we multiply Divinity; that almost all the Church Fathers contradict each other in their writings; which proves that they were not inspired by God.

"All the changes to our religion since Adam,

made by Moses, Solomon, Jesus Christ and finally the Church Fathers, demonstrate that all these religions are nothing but the work of men. God never varies, he is immutable.

"God is everywhere: however the Holy Scriptures say that God seeks Adam in the terrestrial paradise; *Adam ubi es?*[10] God asks, when taking a stroll there, where he converses with the devil on the subject of Job.

"Reason tells me that God is not subject to any passion; however, in *Genesis*, chapter VI, God is made to say that he repents having created man; that his anger was not without effect. But God appears so weak in the Christian religion that man cannot be reduced to the degree he would like: he punishes him by water, then by fire: man remains always the same; he sends his prophets, men are still the same; he has but one son, he sends him, he sacrifices him; however men do not change in any way: how ridiculous the Christian religion makes God out to be!

"Everyone agrees that God knows what must happen during eternity; but God, it is said, does not know what must result from our actions until only after having anticipated that we would abuse his graces and that we would repeat the same actions; this knowledge nonetheless results in this: that God, by having brought us into the world, already knew that we would be infallibly damned and eternally miserable.

"One reads in the Holy Scriptures that God

[10]*Adam ubi es?:* Latin for "Adam, where are you?"

sent his prophets to warn men and to encourage them to change their behavior. Now God, who knows all, was not ignorant that men would not change at all in their conduct. So the Holy Scriptures suppose that God is a liar. Can these ideas be reconciled with the certitude that we participate in God's infinite goodness?

"One supposes that God, who is all powerful, has a dangerous rival in the devil, who takes from him constantly, in spite of himself, three quarters of the small number of men whom he has chosen, for whom his son was sacrificed, without bothering himself with the rest of humankind. What pitiful absurdities!

"According to the Christian religion, we sin because of temptation; it is the devil, one says, who tempts us. All God had to do was to annihilate the devil: we would have been saved; he is either unjust or powerless.

"A rather large number of ministers of the Catholic religion pretend that God gives us the commandments but claim that one would not know how to follow them without the grace God gives to those who please him;[11] and that, however, God punishes those who do not observe them! What a contradiction! What a monstrous impiety!

"Is there anything so miserable as to say that God is vindictive, jealous, angry; to see Catholics addressing their prayers to the saints; as if these saints were everywhere, like God; as if these saints could

[11]those who please him: viz., his ministers and priests.

read men's hearts and hear them?

"What ridiculousness to say that we must do everything for the greatest glory of God! Can the glory of God be augmented by men's imagination, by men's actions? Can they augment anything in him? Is he not sufficient unto himself?

"How could men imagine that Divinity should be more honored, more satisfied, by seeing them eat a herring instead of a lark on a certain day of the week; a bowl of *soupe à l'oignon* instead of soup with bacon in it; a plate of sole rather than a partridge, and that this same Divinity would damn them for all eternity if, on certain days, they preferred soup with bacon in it!

"Weak mortals! you think you can offend God! If you could only offend a king, a prince, who were reasonable, how would that work out? They would despise your weakness and your powerlessness. One proclaims a vengeful God to you, and you are told that vengeance is a crime. What a contradiction! You are assured that forgiving an offense is a virtue and one dares tell you that God avenges himself of an involuntary offense[12] by an eternity of suffering!

"If there is a God, one says, there is worship. However, before the creation of the world, one has to admit that there was a God but no worship. Moreover, since creation, there were beasts who rendered no worship unto God. If there were no men, there would always be God, creatures, and no worship. The queer

[12]Original footnote: Original sin.

habit of men is to judge the actions of God by those that are specific to themselves.

"The Christian religion gives a false idea of God; because human justice, according to the Christian religion, is an emanation of divine justice. Now, according to human justice, we are only able to blame the actions of God towards his son, towards Adam, towards the people one has never preached to, towards the children who die before baptism.

"According to the Christian religion, one must strive towards the greatest perfection. The state of virginity, accordingly, is more perfect than that of marriage: so it is evident that the perfection of the Christian religion tends toward the destruction of the human species. If the efforts, the discourses, of priests succeeded, in sixty or eighty years the human species would be wiped off the face of the earth. Can this be the religion of God?

"Is there anything so absurd as to have God prayed to on one's behalf by priests, monks, or other people? One thinks of God as one thinks of kings.

"What a superabundance of madness it is to believe that God had us born in order that we might do only what is against our nature, only what might make us unhappy, by requiring that we refuse everything that satisfies our senses, the appetites we were born with! What more could an unrelenting tyrant do to persecute us from the time we are born until our dying breath?

"In order to be a perfect Christian, one must

be ignorant and believe blindly; renounce all pleasures, honors, and riches; abandon one's parents and friends, and remain a virgin; in a word, one must do everything that is against our nature. However, that nature surely does not operate except by God's will. What a contrariety that religion posits in a being that is infinitely good and just!

"Given that God is the creator and master of all things, we must employ them all for the usages he designed them for and make use of them for the ends he created them for; as much by reason as by the feelings within ourselves that he gave us, we can recognize his design and purpose and reconcile them with the interests of society established by men, in the countries that we inhabit.

"Man is not made to be lazy: he must occupy himself with something that has for its purpose a particular advantage for himself in line with the general good. God did not want happiness for only a few individuals; he wants happiness for all. We must then mutually provide for ourselves all possible services, provided these services do not destroy any branches of established society; it is this last point that ought to guide us in all our actions. By restricting ourselves in what we do, according to our condition, we fulfill our duties; the rest is but a chimera, an illusion, a prejudice.

"All religions, bar none, are the work of man; there is not one among them that has not had its martyrs, its pretended miracles. What do our own martyrs and miracles prove that is any better than that of other religions?

"In the beginning, religions were founded on fear: thunder, lightning, wind, and hail destroyed the fruit and grain that nourished the first men spread across the surface of the earth; their powerlessness to defend themselves against these events obliged them to have recourse to prayers to what they recognized as more powerful than themselves, and which they believed was bent on tormenting them. Subsequently, ambitious men, towering geniuses, great politicians, born in different centuries, in divers regions, took advantage of peoples' credulity and announced gods that are often bizarre; fantastic tyrants established cults and undertook to form societies that they could become the leaders and legislators of; they understood that, to maintain these societies, it was necessary that each member should often sacrifice his passions, his personal pleasures, for the good of others. From there, the need to make believe in equivalent recompenses to be hoped for and punishments to be feared, which persuaded the people to perform these sacrifices.

"These politicians therefore came up with religions. They all promise rewards and announce punishments that engage a large number of men to resist the natural penchant they have to take another man's property, wife, daughter; to wreak vengeance, to lie, and to blacken the reputation of their neighbor, in order to make their own reputation stand out. Honor was afterwards associated with religions. This being,[13] every bit as chimerical as them, every bit as useful to society's happiness as it is in every other

[13]This being: scil., God.

particular, was imagined to contain within the same limits, and by the same principles, a certain number of other men.

"There is a God, the creator and mover of all that exists, we have no doubt about it; we are part of it all, and everything we do is in consequence of the first principles of movement that God set in motion. Everything is worked out in advance and necessary; nothing is done by chance. Three dice thrown by a gambler must infallibly add up to one score or another, with regards to the arrangement of the dice in his cup, according to the force and movement he gives to them. The toss of the dice is a metaphor for all the actions in our life. One die strikes another, giving a necessary movement to it; one movement leads to another movement, resulting finally in a score. In the same way man, by his first movement, by his first action, is determined invincibly to make a second action, and a third, etc.

"Because to say that a man wants a thing simply because he wants it, is to say nothing at all, it supposes that emptiness produces an effect. It is evident that there is a motive, a reason, that determines him to want that thing, and from one reason to next, each reason determined by the one coming before it, a man's will is invincibly forced to take such or such an action over the course of his life, the end of which is like that of a toss of the die.

"Let us love God, not because he demands it of us, but because he is sovereignly good, and let us fear only men and their laws. Let us respect the laws, because they are needed for the public weal, which each of us participates in.

"There you have it, madame," added the abbot T***, "what my friendship for you has snatched from me on the subject of religions. It is the fruit of twenty years of labor, long nights, and meditations, during which I have sought with good faith to be able to distinguish the truth from a lie.

"Let us conclude, then, my dear friend, that the pleasures we enjoy, you and me, are pure and innocent because they harm neither God nor men, because of the secrecy and the decency that we employ in our conduct. Without these two conditions, I admit that we would cause a scandal, and that we would be criminals with respect to society: our example could seduce young hearts destined, by their families, by their birth, to employments of utility to the public good, which they perhaps might neglect to assume in order to follow instead the torrent of pleasures."

"But," replied Madame C***, "if our pleasures are innocent, as I conceive them to be presently, why not, on the contrary, instruct everybody in the proper way to enjoy them in the same way? Why not share with our friends, with our fellow citizens, the fruit you have culled from your metaphysical meditations, given that nothing could contribute more to their peace and happiness? Haven't you told me a hundred times that there's no greater pleasure than making people happy?"

"That is true what I said to you, madame," replied the abbot T., "but we must be careful not to reveal to sots truths they would not understand or that they would abuse. They must be understood by people who can think and whose passions are in such equilibrium that they are not enthralled by any one of them. This type of person is very rare: out of a hundred thousand people, only twenty are in the habit of thinking; and of these twenty, you would be hard pressed to find four who think actually on their own, and who are not swept away by some dominant passion. From which it follows that one must be extremely circumspect as regards the type of truths that we have examined today.

"Given that few people see the need to be bothered with the happiness of their neighbors in order to be assured of the happiness they seek for themselves, only a few people should be given clear proofs of the insufficiency of religions, which ensures the behavior of a large number of men and keeps them in their duties and in their observation of the rules that, fundamentally, are only useful for the good of society, under the veil of religion, because of the fear of punishment and the hope for eternal reward which religions proclaim. It is this fear and this hope that guide the weak: the number of them is large. Honor, human laws, and public interest are what guide thinking men: the number of them is, in all honesty, quite small."

After M. the abbot T*** had stopped talking, Madame C*** thanked him in glowing terms. "You're adorable, my dear friend," she said to him, giving him a big hug. "How fortunate I am to know and to love a man who thinks as sanely as you do! Be assured that I'll never abuse your trust in me, and that

I'll follow the soundness of your principles to the letter."

After several kisses mutually given and received once again, and which annoyed me to no end, because of the awkward position I found myself in, my pious director of conscience and his docile proselyte went downstairs to the room where they were accustomed to receive visitors and socialize. I promptly returned to my room, where I locked myself in. One instant later, someone came calling on me on behalf of Madame C***. I asked that it be communicated to Madame C*** that I had not slept a wink the night before and that I begged to be allowed to rest for another few hours. I used this time to put down on paper everything I had just heard.

Our days passed quickly in the countryside, in reciprocal testimonies of friendship, when my mother showed up suddenly, one morning, to announce to me that our trip to Paris was arranged for the following day. We dined together, my mother and I and the kind Madame C***, whom I left as tears rolled down my cheeks. This adorable woman, perhaps one of a kind, overwhelmed me with caresses and gave me the most sage advice, while sparing me useless and oppressive pettiness and smalltalk. M. the abbot T*** had gone to a neighboring village where he was supposed to spend one week. I didn't see him. We returned to Volnot where we passed the night. Everything was ready for our trip. We boarded a *post chaise* the following day, which took us to Lyon, from which the diligence carried us to Paris.

I mentioned earlier that my mother was determined to make this trip because a considerable sum of money was owed to her by a merchant of her acquaintance, and that our entire fortune depended on his payment of this sum. On the other hand, my mother was in debt herself, because her business was languishing. Before leaving Volnot, she had left all her affairs in the hands of her attorney, a relative, who ended up by losing them. My mother learned that everything she owned had been confiscated from her house; to add insult to injury, that same day she was told that her debtor in Paris, burdened with debt and too actively pursued by a multitude of lenders, had declared complete but fraudulent bankruptcy. Most people don't do well when so many disappointments hit them all at once: my poor mother succumbed to them; a malignant fever did her in after one week.

And there I was smack dab in the middle of Paris, made to shift for myself, without relatives, without friends, pretty, so I'm told, instructed in many things, but with no practical knowledge of the ways of the world.

My mother, before she died, gave to me a purse, in which I discovered four hundred *louis d'or*; being otherwise well possessed of clothing and linen, I considered myself rich. My first instinct was however to get me to a convent and become a nun; but on further reflection, remembering what I had suffered previously in such a place, combined with the counsels of a lady, my neighbor, with whom I had scraped together the beginnings of an acquaintance, I was dissuaded from this fatal plan.

This lady, who went by the name of Bois-Laurier, had a room next to the one I occupied in a furnished hotel. She was kind enough not to leave me alone in the first month that followed my mother's death, and I owe her eternal thanks for the attentions she showered on me in order to ameliorate the afflictions I was oppressed with. Madame Bois-Laurier was, as you know, a woman constrained by necessity, in her youth, to satisfy the misbehavior of public libertines, and who, following the example of so many others before her, assumed at that time incognito the role of an honest woman, with the help of a lifetime annuity that she had secured for herself by savings from her first jobs.

However, the afflictions that devoured me gave way to reflections. The future frightened me; I opened up to my friend; I confided in her the state of my finances and the fear I had for myself in such a situation. She had a sound mind tempered by experience.

"How very silly you are," she said to me one morning, "to be so vividly disquieted over a future that's no more certain for the wealthy than it is for the poorest, and which should appear less critical to you than to another! Is a girl with your virtue, your waist, your face ever put out, for what little prudence or comportment she adds to the mix? No, mademoiselle, don't you worry your pretty little face: I'll find you what you need, perhaps even a good husband; for it seems to me that your obsession is to tend toward the sacrament of marriage. Alas! my poor child, you've little idea of the true value of what you wish for there! In any case, leave everything to me; a forty-year-old woman, who has the experience of a fifty-year-old, knows what a girl like you needs. I'll act like your mother," she added, "and as your chaperon when you saunter out in the world; starting today, I'll introduce you to my uncle B***, who's supposed to come and see me: he's a rich financier, an honest man, who'll find a good match for you in no time."

I jumped up to embrace Bois-Laurier, whom I thanked with all my heart, and I vowed in good faith that the assuring tone with which she spoke to me persuaded me that my future fortune was certain.

My how a girl without experience, with a great deal of self-esteem, is stupid! M. abbot T***'s lessons had really opened my eyes on the role we must play here below, in view of God and the laws of men; but I had no knowledge of the ways of the world.

Everything I saw and heard appeared full of the probity I had found in Madame C*** and the abbot T***, and I believed Father Dirrag to be the only bad man in the world. Poor innocent me! I was grossly mistaken!

The financier B*** arrived at Madame Bois-Laurier's at around five o'clock in the evening. As might be expected, the first quarter of an hour of his visit was spent talking about things entirely unrelated to me. His "niece" was too clever not to put the uncle in a state of calm that left him nothing to fear from the effect of my charms, which she said were dangerous. It took a long time. Towards seven o'clock, I was presented to M. B***, to whom, on entering, I made a deep curtsey which he didn't bother to reciprocate by rising. He had me sit down, however, on a chair, beside an armchair on which he was half-reclining, in his shirt sleeves, pushing out his big belly, and he received me with the air and the manners common among people of his station; everything appeared admirable to me nevertheless, including the praises he bestowed on the firmness of my thigh, which he touched with his hand brutally, squeezing it with all his strength, to the point that I had to cry out.

"My niece's spoken to me about you," he said to me without paying any attention to the pain he had just caused me; "What the devil! you've got nice eyes, teeth, a firm thigh! Oh! we can do something with you. As early as tomorrow, I'll have you dine with one of my colleagues who has a room this size full of gold; I know his personality: he'll be in love with you at first sight; treat him nice; I tell you he's a *bon vivant* and I'm sure you'll like him. Goodbye, my dear children," he added while getting up and buttoning his vest. "Give me a kiss the both of you, and you, look on me as if I were your father. You, niece, send word to my hideaway that a meal should be prepared for us."

As soon as our financier had exited, Madame Bois-Laurier confided in me how delighted she was that he had found me to his taste. "He's an informal man," she told me, "with an excellent heart and an essential friend. Let me take care of everything: I've taken a sincere liking to you; just do what I tell you, don't act the prude, and I'll see to it you make your fortune."

I supped with my new mentor, who adroitly sounded me out as regards my manner of thinking and the ways in which I had conducted myself to date.

Her effusion of feelings for me made me reciprocate. I chatted more than I wished to. At first she was alarmed to learn that I had never had a lover before; but she was reassured once I had persuaded her, by responses to questions she subtly extracted from me, that I knew the value of love's pleasures and that I had drawn an honest opinion of them. Bois-Laurier kissed me on the cheek, and caressed me; she did all she could to convince me to sleep with her in the same bed. I thanked her, but I retired to my own room, my mind extremely occupied by the good fortune that was waiting for me.

Parisians are a lively and affectionate bunch! The next morning, my obliging neighbor came and proposed to me to have my hair curled, to make use of a chambermaid, to doll myself up; but mourning for my mother prevented me from accepting these offers, besides I was still wearing my little nightcap. The curious Bois-Laurier made an endless number of naughty little remarks and observations, and made a thorough inventory of all my charms, with her eyes and with her hands, giving me a shirt that she wanted to put on me herself: "You little scamp!" she said to me after reflecting, "I think you're getting dressed without having first washed your snatch; where's your bidet, by the way?"

"I don't know, to be honest," I said to her, "what do you mean by *bidet*."

"How's that?" she said to me, "no bidet? Don't ever be so vain as to think you can do without an item as indispensable to a fresh-looking girl as a clean shirt. For today, I'll be happy to loan you mine; but tomorrow, without hesitation, see to it that you go out and buy yourself one." Bois-Laurier's bidet was then brought to my room; she plopped me down on it, and, despite all I could say or do, this officious woman, while laughing and acting like a madwoman, took it upon herself to wash abundantly what she called my little *snatch*. Lavender water was even applied to it. How little I suspected the party it was being primped for, and the motive of this exact *lavabo*!

Towards noon, a respectable *fiacre* conducted us to M. B***'s hideaway, where he was waiting together with M. R***, his colleague and friend. This latter man was from thirty-eight to forty years old, had a somewhat good-looking face, and was richly dressed, affecting to show us, one after the other, his rings, his snuffboxes, his cases, playing the role of an important man. He deigned nevertheless to approach me and, holding both my hands, looked me attentively in the face: "She's pretty, by golly!" he exclaimed; "On my honor! she's charming, and I want to make her my little woman."

"Oh! sir, you do me such great honor, thank you *so* much" I rejoined, "and if..."

"No, no," he interrupted me, "Don't be embarrassed: I'll arrange everything in such a way that you'll be happy."

It was announced that lunch was served; we

sat down at the table. Bois-Laurier, who knew the rigamarole and the accustomed phrases to be used at these sorts of meals, was charming. No matter how hard she tried to encourage me, I felt completely out of place, and I didn't say a word, or when I did speak it was using expressions that sounded so sullen to the two financiers that the former liveliness of M. R*** evaporated: he looked at me with large eyes that suggested the idea he had of my mind: ordinarily one does not socialize with people who do not think and act as we do. However, several glasses of Champagne soon repaired, in R***'s imagination, the wrongs that the sterility of my conversation had planted there. He became more pressing, and I more docile. He imposed on me with his comfortable attitude; his thieving hands flitted about, a little bit everywhere; and my fear of offending him for acting in a way I took to be normal for a Parisian prevented me from daring to stand up to him seriously. I believed myself to be all the more authorized to let things go their natural way when I saw on a sofa, at the other end of the room, M. B*** running his hands a bit more cavalierly over madame his niece's attractions. In the end, I defended myself so poorly against R***'s little endeavors that he had no doubt in his mind about succeeding, in the end, if he tried more serious ones. He proposed that we go and sit down on the couch that was facing the sofa.

"Sounds good to me, sir," I said to him simply; "I think we'll be more comfortable, and I'm concerned lest you tire yourself out too much in your current position, at my knees." (He had just, in fact, positioned himself there.) Immediately he got up and carried me over to the couch.

With this action of his, I noticed that M. B*** and his niece were leaving the room; I wanted to get up and follow them; but the enterprising R***, declaring to me in so many words that he was crazy about me and that he wanted to make my fortune, had trussed up with one hand my shirt as far as my waist and with the other hand had pulled out from his trousers his stiff and spirited member; his knee was passed between my thighs, which he spread as best he could, and he was getting ready to satisfy his violent urge when, bringing my eyes to bear on the monster that I was menaced with, I noticed it had about the same physiognomy as the aspergillum Father Dirrag employed to exorcise the impure spirits out of his penitents' body.

I recalled then all the dangers that M. the abbot T*** had put into my head as to the nature of the operation I was being menaced with. My docility flip-flopped immediately into fury; I seized the redoubtable R*** by the tie, and, with outstretched arm, I held him in a position that put him out of reach of the thing he was making every effort to gain. Then, with my eyes fixed, for fear of surprise, on the head of the enemy that I was afraid of being threaded by, I called out at the top of my lungs for Madame Bois-Laurier's assistance, who, whether she was in on R***'s plans or not, could not help but run to my aid and blame his behavior.

Furious at the affront I had just received by this R***, I was on the verge of tearing his eyes out; I reproached him, in the most heated terms, for his temerity. M. B*** had joined Bois-Laurier; together the two of them could barely keep me from escaping their grip and throwing myself at R***, when this latter man, after having calmly put the critical furniture back into its den, broke the silence by letting out a huge burst of laughter.

"By golly! the little country wench," he said, pretending he was just playing with me, "you've got to agree that I got you, eh? You didn't seriously think that I wanted...? Oh! what a piece of work is a girl from the countryside, who hasn't the least idea how things work in polite society! Imagine for a moment! my dear B***," he continued, "I laid mademoiselle down on the couch, I lifted her skirts, I showed her my...; the little prude had no idea there was anything irregular in all this business! She played the *imp*, you two entered: that's all there is to it, while this beautiful little girl stands there convulsing as you can see; don't you think there's something to die laughing about?" he added doubling down in laughter. "But, Bois-Laurier," he started up again suddenly with great seriousness in his tone of voice, "I implore you not to put me through this kind of stupid thing again; I'm not at all suited for playing the schoolmaster or professor of civility, and you'd do well to make mademoiselle here know how she should act before introducing her to men like B*** and me."

My arms, I swear to you, dropped to my sides during this singular harangue. Listening to R***, my mouth opened, I looked at him with dazed eyes, and I didn't say a word.

B*** disappeared with R*** without my even

noticing them disappear, so to speak, and I stood there like a stupid girl in Bois-Laurier's arms, who also mumbled between her teeth certain little words and phrases that were intended to make me understand I should not feel as though I had done anything wrong. We climbed back into the *fiacre*, and we returned home.

It didn't take long for me to feel overwhelmed by the agitation of my senses. On arrival at the hotel, I broke down sobbing. My chaste companion, who was not comfortable with the ideas that lingered with me of my adventure, didn't leave my side; she sought to persuade me that men were always curious to understand to what point a girl whom they have a desire to marry knows about amorous pleasures. The conclusion of her fine reasoning was that prudence should have led me to affect more ignorance, and that she saw with sadness that my liveliness had perhaps deprived me of my fortune.

I responded to her, with warmth, that I was not so little informed of the ways of the world as to be ignorant of what the shameful R*** was intending to do to me. I added rather dryly that the greatest fortune in the world could never tempt me, given the cost. Carried away by my agitation, I recounted for her then what I had seen happen between Father Dirrag and Mademoiselle Eradice, and the lessons I had received, on this subject, by the abbot T*** and Madame C***.

Finally, one thing led to another, and the crafty Bois-Laurier succeeded in drawing out of me my entire story. The details I gave her made her change her tune; if I had previously appeared to her so little instructed in the habits and practices of the world, she was not a little surprised now by my deep knowledge of morality, metaphysics, and religion.

Bois-Laurier has an excellent heart. "How enchanted I am," she told me, embracing me tightly, "to know a girl like you! You've just opened my eyes to mysteries that have caused me a world of hurt in my life; reflections that I continue to make on my past behavior trouble my sleep. Who should fear more than me the punishments we are menaced with for crimes that you've demonstrated to me are involuntary? The beginning of my life was a web of horrors; but, even though it may cost me my self-esteem, I owe you a confidence for a confidence, a lesson for a lesson.

"Listen, then, my dear Thérèse, to the story of my adventures; by instructing you on the capriciousness of men, which it's good that you should know, it can also contribute to firm up in you the idea that in effect vice and virtue depend on temperament and education."

AND WITH THAT, THIS WOMAN BEGAN TO TELL ME HER STORY.

The Story of Bois-Laurier

You see in me, dear Thérèse, a singular being. I am not a man, not a woman, not a daughter, not a widow, not married. I have been a libertine by profession, but I am still a virgin. With such an opener, you must take me doubtless for a madwoman: a little patience, I beg you, and you will have the key to the enigma. Nature, capricious in my view, has planted insurmountable obstacles along the road of pleasures that leads a girl from maidenhead to womanhood: an energetic membrane obstructs the way with enough exactitude that the swiftest and finest arrow ever to be found in Cupid's quiver was incapable of striking its target; and, what might surprise you even more, one has never been able to compel me to submit to an operation that could have made me a skilled lover, even though, in an effort to overcome my repugnance, I was given the examples, at every moment, of an infinite number of young ladies who, in the same situation, were subjected to this ordeal.

Destined from the most tender age of childhood to become a courtesan, this defect, which seemed like it should have gotten in the way of my success at this shameful profession, has been, on the contrary, its principal driver. You should understand then that, when I said that my adventures would instruct you in men's caprices, I did not intend to speak to you about the different attitudes of sexual desire, so infinitely varied by nature, so to speak, that each man has insofar as he interacts with women. All the different nuances of galant attitudes have been documented with great energy by the celebrated Pierre Arétin, who lived in the XVth century, such that there is nothing new under the sun to be said on the subject today. There is no question then, in what I am about to tell you, how many of these bents of fantasy, how many of these bizarre indulgences exist, that a large number of men insist on demanding from us and that, by predilection or by a certain congenital defect, stand in for normal intercourse. I will begin my story now.

I never met my father or mother. A woman of Paris, named Lefort, lodged in a bourgeois neighborhood, with whom I had been raised as if I were her daughter, took me aside one mysterious day in particular, to tell me what I am about to tell you (I was fifteen years old then):

"Your not my daughter," said Madame Lefort; "it's time I instructed you as to your background and position. At the age of six, you was lost on the streets of Paris; I took you in, nourished you and supported you charitably to this day, without ever being able to discover who your parents is, in spite of my efforts.

"You must notice I'm not rich, though I spared nothing as far as your learning is concerned. It's up to you now to be the instrument of your fortune. What I'm about to tell you," she added, "is all you needs to know in order to get on in the world: Your very purdy, with a better-looking *figur* than a girl your age *ordnarily* has. M. the president de M***, my protector and my neighbor, is in love with you. You decide, Manon, what you wants me to tell him; but I got to tell you if you doesn't accept without reservation his offer I'm entrusted to tell you, you must leave my house today, because I'm not able to feed you or clothe you any longer."

This excruciating little talk, and Madame Lefort's conclusion to it, terrified me. I burst out in tears. It made no difference: I needed to decide. After several preliminary explanations by her, I promised to do all that was asked of me, whereby Madame Lefort assured me that she would always care for me and assume the sweet name of mother.

The following morning, she instructed me fully on the duties inherent in the arrangement I was about to embrace and the particular procedures I needed to follow with M. the president. Then she had me get completely undressed, washed my body from head to toe, curled my hair, made my coiffure, and dressed me in clothes much more proper than I was accustomed to wearing.

At fifteen minutes passed noon, we called on M. the president. He was a tall, lean man, whose wrinkled, yellow face was buried in a very long and very ample square peruke. This respectable personage, after having made us sit down, said gravely, while addressing his words to my mother: "So this is the young person in question, then? She looks quite nice: I have always told you that she had promise of becoming pretty in the face and figure; and so far the money has been well spent; but you are sure at least that she is still a virgin?" he added. "Let us see for ourselves, Madame Lefort." As soon as he said this, my good mother made me sit on the edge of a bed and, lying down on my back, she lifted up my skirts and proceeded to spread open my thighs when M. the president said to her in a brusk tone of voice: “Eh! not like that, madame; why are women always obsessed with showing their front side! Eh! no, turn her over...”

“Ah! monseigneur, I beg your pardon,” exclaimed my mother; “I thought you was wanting to see... Right! get up, Manon,” she said to me; “put your knee on this chair, and lean your body forward as far as you can.”

Me, just like a victim before the sacrifice, with eyes lowered, I did what was asked of me. My honorable mother lifted up my dress to my hips while I stood in this position, and while M. the president having approached, I felt her open the lips of my …, into which monseigneur attempted to introduce his finger, touching, but unable to penetrate.

“That is quite good,” he said to my mother, “and I am content: I can see clearly that she is a virgin. Now, make her stay still like that without moving: slap her a few times with your hand on the buttocks.” The order was given. A profound silence ensued. My mother, holding up my skirts and my shirt with her left hand, slapped me lightly with her right hand on my butt. Curious to see what the president was doing, I turned my head around just enough: I saw him positioned two steps away from my derriere, one knee on the ground, holding his lorgnette fixed on my posterior with the one hand, and, with his other hand, shaking between his legs something dark and flabby that for the life of him he could not make hard.

I don’t know know if he finished the job or

not; but finally, after a quarter of an hour in a position I could no longer hold, monseigneur got up and walked back to his armchair, while vacillating on his old bony legs. He gave to my mother a purse in which he said she would find the promised one hundred *louis d'or*; and having honored me with a kiss on the cheek, he announced to me that he would see to it that I was lacking in nothing, provided that I was well-behaved, and that he would let me know when he should have need of me.

As soon as my mother and I returned to our lodgings, continued Madame Bois-Laurier, I made serious reflections on what I had learned and seen in the last twenty-four hours, in the same way as you had after Father Dirrag's flogging of Mademoiselle Eradice. I went over in my head everything that had been said and done in Madame Lefort's house since my childhood, and I was collecting my thoughts in order to come to some reasonable conclusion when my mother entered my room and put an end to my reveries.

"I got nothing more to hide from you, my dear Manon," she told me, hugging me, "cause you now been introduced to the duties of a profession I exercised with some distinction for twenty years. Listen up attentively then to what I still got to tell you, and by your docility in following my advice, put yourself in a position to repair the wrong the president's done you. It was by his command," continued my mother, "I abducted you when you was eight years old. He paid me, since then, a very modest pension, which I used, plus some of my own money, for your learning. He promised me he'd give us both one hundred louis when you was old enough for him to take your virginity; but if this dirty old man counted on his host, and if his rusty, worn-out, wrinkled old tool puts him *outta* commission to try that adventure, – is that our fault? Anyways, he gave me the one hundred louis he owed me; but don't worry, my dear Manon, I'll help you make much more money than that. Your young, purdy, and unknown; I'll, to please you, spend this money to fix you up; and if you lets me guide you, I'll help you make, for you yourself, as much profit as ten or twelve of my lady friends made."

After a thousand other words of this sort, through which I understood that my good mother was starting off by appropriating to herself the one hundred louis given to her by the president, the conditions of our pact were such that she would begin to advance me this money, that she would pay herself back from the fruits of my first labors, and that finally we would split, conscientiously, the profits of our business.

Lefort had an inexhaustible source of good acquaintances in Paris. In less than six weeks, I was presented to more than twenty friends of hers, all who failed, one after the other, in the project of culling the first fruits of my virginity. Fortunately, because of the good order that Madame Lefort put in the arrangement of her affairs, she had taken the precaution of have herself paid in advance for the pleasures of a job that was impracticable. I was afraid one day even that a fat doctor of the Sorbonne, who persisted in wanting to enjoy the ten louis he had spent, would have died nearly or would have *broken my charm.*

These twenty athletes were followed by more than five hundred others, in the space of five years. Men of the Clergy, Nobility of the Sword,[14] Nobility of the Robe, and Finance placed me, one after the other, in the most elaborate of poses: pointless endeavors! Either sacrifice was done at the temple door or the tip of the knife was blunted: the victim could not be immolated.

Finally the inviolability of my maidenhead made too much noise and was heard even by the police, who seemed to want to put an end to the progress of these tests. I was warned in advance; and we judged, Madame Lefort and me, that prudence required that we should disappear for a while, thirty leagues from Paris.

At the end of three months, the heat had died down. An exempt officer from this same police, an accomplice and friend of Madame Lefort, was charged with calming spirits, by means of a sum of twelve *louis d'or* that we paid him. We returned to Paris with new projects in mind.

My mother, who had insisted for a long time on what an operation by a bistoury would have done for me, changed her mind finally; she found in my congenital deformity an unalterable fund that produced a large revenue – without ever being reaped, with no need for *clary sage*,[15] without fear of bearing children, and without fear of contracting *ecclesiastic*

[14]Nobility of the Sword: the knights, the feudal lords, the true nobility.

[15] clary sage: *orvale* in French, it is said to induce a miscarriage.

rheums.[16] As for my sexual satisfaction, I had my fill, my dear Thérèse, as necessary, in the same way you satisfy yourself.

However, continued Bois-Laurier, we put on new appearances, and we guided ourselves by new principles. After returning from our voluntary exile, our first concern was to change quarters; and without saying a word to the president, we relocated ourselves to the faubourg Saint-Germain.

The first person I met was that of a certain baroness who, after having worked during her youth to good effect and in concert with a countess, her sister, to satisfy the pleasures of young libertines, had become the directress of the house owned by a rich American in Paris, on whom she lavished what remained of her outdated charms, which he paid over and above their true value for. Another American, a friend of this last one, saw me and fell in love: we came to an agreement. The secret that I confided in him as to my situation charmed him rather than turned him off. The poor man brought out from between his hands the infamous little Penis Sleeve.[17] He felt assured that between my own hands he had no fear of a relapse. My new lover from *across the ocean* had made a vow to limit himself to small favors only; but he added to the execution a singular tic. It was his desire to have me seated next to him on the sofa, naked up to the navel; and while I jerked him off

[16]ecclesiastical rheums: presumably the "French disease" or some other type of venereal disease.

[17]Penis Sleeve: a device to help keep a penis erect.

and while he came, it was necessary that I be complaisant enough to allow a chambermaid, whom he had assigned to me, to busy herself by cutting small hairs off my bush. Without this bizarre appliance, I believe that the vigor of ten arms like my own would not have been able to make my man's machine hard, let alone extract a drop of elixir from it.

Included among the number of these men with sexual fantasies was the lover of Minette, the third sister of the baroness. This girl had beautiful eyes; she was tall, rather shapely, but ugly in the face, dark haired, thin, simpering, pretending to be witty and have sensibilities when she had in fact neither of these things. It was the beauty of her voice that had procured for her a long string of adorers. Her lover at the time was moved by this talent of hers, and the mere tones of melodious voice by this female Orpheus had the virtue of rocking that lover's boat and whipping him up into a froth.

One day, after the three of us had partaken of an ample libertine dinner, during which one of us had sung, small jokes were made on the deformity of my...; and all imaginable craziness was said and done: we settled back on the large bed; there, our various charms were put on display, mine were found to be admirable to look at; the lover got started, he placed Minette on the edge of the bed, pulled up her skirts, stuck his prick in her and asked her to sing. The docile Minette, after a short prelude, intones an aria with a tempo in triple time; the lover pulls out, pushes in, pushes in again, always in time: his lips seem to keep the beat, while he slaps her on the butt to mark the rhythm. I watch on, I listen while laughing myself to tears, lying on the same bed. Everything was going along just swimmingly until the point when the sensuous Minette, beginning to enjoy herself as things progressed, sings off key, out of tune, loses the beat: a *flat* is substituted for a *natural.*

"Ah! bitch!" our zealot for good music cried out suddenly, "you have torn my eardrum; that flat note has penetrated me all the way to the linchpin, it throws everything off kilter; look," he said, pulling himself out of her, "look at what your damned *flat* note has done!" Alas! the poor devil had gone soft, the wand that had been keeping the beat was reduced to a limp rag.

Feeling desperate, my friend made incredible efforts to put some life back into the actor, but the most tender kisses, the most lascivious touches were all for nought; they could not return elasticity to the languishing part. "Ah! my dear friend," she exclaimed, "don't abandon me: it's my love for you, it's the pleasure I was feeling that upset my voice; will you leave me now at this happy moment? Manon, my dear Manon, help me: show him your little cunt; that'll put some life back into it, that'll restore me too, because I'm dying, if this doesn't come to a happy end. Put her, my dear Bibi," she said to her lover, "into the sexy position that you put my sister the countess into sometimes; Manon's friendship will answer for me in her willingness to please."

During all this time, I hadn't stopped laughing, to the point that I was losing my breath. In all honesty, has one ever seen such a need for singing and keeping the beat with such a wand? And can one ever imagine that a flat note instead of a natural one could make such a mess of things and make a man go soft?

I understood that the sister of the baroness was prepared to do everything she could to please her lover, less for sexual desire than to retain him in his thralls by the indulgences she made him pay dearly for; but I was still unclear as to the role that the countess played, whom I was asked to double for... I was soon filled in. Here's what it entailed:

The two lovers lie on my stomach, under which they place three or four cushions that keep my buttocks elevated; then they pull up my skirts to just below my hips, my head resting against the head of the bed. Minette stretches out on her back, places her head between my thighs, my bush next to her face, which acts as her toupet. Bibi lifts Minette's skirts and shirt, lies down on her and holds himself up by his arms. Notice, my dear Thérèse, that in this position M. Bibi has in view, at one foot from his face, his lover's face, my bush, my buttocks and all the rest. This time, he did without the music. He kissed indistinctly all that was before him, face, ass, mouth, with no marked preference: it was all the same to him; his prick, guided by Minette's hand, regained quickly enough its elasticity and found its place again. That's when the sparks started flying in earnest: the lover pushed, Minette swore, bit, moved her jaw with unparalleled agility; as for me, I continued laughing myself to tears, while watching with both eyes the work that was going on behind me; finally, after a rather long time at it, the two lovers swooned and were swimming in a sea of delights.

Some time later, I was introduced to a bishop whose odd habit was louder, which was more dangerous in terms of scandal and for the tympanum of the ear, particularly a more refined one. Imagine for yourself, either because of a certain penchant, or by constitutional defect, from the moment His Greatness felt he was approaching ecstasy, he bellowed and shouted at the top of his lungs: “Hey! Hey! Hey!” while increasing the pitch in proportion to the amount of pleasure he was feeling; to the effect that one could calculate the degree of excitement that the big, fat prelate felt by how loud he bellowed: “Hey! Hey! Hey!” A noisy racket that, at the moment of the monseigneur’s discharge, could have been heard a thousand paces away, if it were not for the precaution taken by his valet who put mattresses against the doors and windows of the episcopal apartment.

I would not be finished if I didn’t paint a picture for you of all the bizarre tastes, the singular habits I have encountered among men, independently of the divers postures they demand of their women during *coitus*.

One day I was introduced, through a small door at the rear, to a very rich nobleman, who had been visited, for fifty years running, each morning by a new girl. He opened the door to his apartment himself. Forewarned as to the *etiquette* that should be observed at this old engrained lecher’s place, from the moment I entered, I stepped out of my skirts and removed my top. Thus naked, I went to stick my ass in his face, for him to kiss, while he sat in an armchair with a serious look on his face.

"Now run, little girl, fast" he said to me, holding his package in his hand, which he shook with all his strength, while in the other hand was a fistful of birch rod, which he simply menaced my buttocks with. I began to run, he followed me; we did five or six laps round the room, while he shouted like the devil: "Run, you bitch, run!" Finally he fell, in a swoon, back into his armchair; I got dressed, he gave me two louis, and I left.

Another man made me sit on the edge of a chair, naked to the waist. In this position, to please him, sometimes to please myself, I had to service myself by rubbing a *dildo* over my clitoris, to make myself horny. Seated in a similar position in front of me, at the other end of the room, he worked with his hand at the same labor, his eyes fixed on my movements, and singularly attentive not to finish his job until he perceived that, by my languor, I had climaxed.

A third man (he used to be a physician) gave no hint of virility until after one hundred blows by a whip that I applied to his backside, while one of my companions, on her knees in front of him, with bared chest, used her hands to stimulate the erectile nerve of this modern Asclepius, from whom finally the spirits emerged that, put into motion by flogging, had been forced to make an appearance in his nether region. It was in this way that we made him, my comrade and me, by different operations, eject the balm of life. Such was the mechanism by which this doctor assured us that one could restore a worn-out old man, an impotent, and make a sterile woman pregnant.

A fourth man (he was a courtier used to debauchery and given to sensuality) had me visit him with one of my companions. We found him in his bureau surrounded by mirrors, which were disposed in such a way that every one of them faced a couch covered in crimson velvet that was placed in the middle of the room. "You are charming, adorable women," said the courtier to us affectionately; "however you will not take it amiss if I do not fuck you... It will be, if you are okay with this, one of my valets, a handsome boy, a strapping youth, who will have what it takes to play with you. What can I tell you, my beautiful children," he added, "one must know how to love one's friends, warts and all, and I have one, which is to enjoy myself only with the idea that I form while watching others enjoy themselves. Besides, it gets messy when... Eh! would it not be pitiful if a man like me were to act the ape to some big ugly peasant!"

After this preliminary discourse, pronounced in a sweet tone of voice, he had his valet enter the room who was wearing a short satin, flesh-colored waistcoat, otherwise dressed for battle. My companion was reclining on the couch, her skirts duly raised by the valet, who then helped me to get naked from the waist up. It was all done stiffly and with restraint. The master, in his armchair, looked on and held his limp tool in hand. The valet, on the contrary, who had dropped his pants down as far as his knees and wrapped the lower part of his shirt tails around his lower back, exposed one of the most brilliant cocks imaginable. He waited for instructions from his master, who announced that he could begin. As soon as the well-endowed valet climbed on my comrade, he stuck his peter in and remained motionless. His buttocks were visible.

"If you would not mind, mademoiselle," said our courtier to me, "place yourself on the other side of the couch and stimulate that full bountiful pair of balls that hang down between the legs of my man, who is, as you can see, a very strong Lorrainian." After having performed this, naked, as I said, from the waist up, the organizer of the party told his valet that he could continue. This latter immediately pushed and pulled, repeatedly with an admirable mobility of buttocks: my hand followed their movements, never letting go his two enormous *eyesores*. The master looked at them in his mirrors, which gave him different pictures, from various angles. In the end, he succeeded in making his tool hard, which he shook with vigor; he felt that the moment of sexual delight was near. "You can finish up now," he said to his valet. This latter redoubled his efforts; the two of them finally fell into a swoon and released the divine essence. Dear Thérèse, said Bois-Laurier while continuing her story, I'm reminded of a pleasant adventure, which happened to me that same day, with three *Capuchins*: it will give you an idea of the exactitude by which these good Fathers observe their vow of chastity.

After having left the courtier's residence, and said goodbye to my companion, as I was turning the first corner of the street to climb into a *fiacre* that was waiting for me, I ran into Dupuis, a friend of my mother's, worthy emulator of my mother's business, but who operated in a more hush-hush world.

"Ah! my dear Manon," she said to me while approaching, "how delighted I am to bump into you! You do know that I've the honor of procuring for almost all our monks in Paris. I'm getting the feeling that those dogs intend to drive me crazy today; they're all in *rut*. Since this morning, I've procured for them nine new girls from the provinces, in divers rooms and quarters of Paris, and I've been running, for the last four hours, trying to find a tenth girl for three venerable Capuchins still waiting for me in a *fiacre* parked on the street, just outside my hideaway. You must, Manon, do me the favor of coming with me; they're good little devils, they'll amuse you." It was all I could do to tell Dupuis what she already knew – that I was not monk meat, that those types of gentlemen are not content with the pleasures derived of fantasy, of girls with a small vagina, but that they needed, on the contrary, girls with very liberal openings.

"Goodness gracious!" Dupuis replied, "I find it admirable that you're concerned for the sexual pleasure of these sons of bitches; alls I need to do is find them a girl; the rest is their business. Come on, look at these six louis they put in my hand: three are for you; so, will you come with me?" Curiosity as well as self-interest won me over. We climbed into my *fiacre*, and we rode to somewhere near Montmartre, to Dupuis' hideaway.

A moment later our three Capuchins entered

who, little accustomed to enjoying a piece of ass as fresh as I appeared to be, rushed at me like three famished dogs. I was standing at the time, one foot resting on a chair, unfastening one of my garters. One of them, the one with a red beard and vile breath, came near me and planted a kiss on my mouth; he was determined to try and penetrate it with his tongue. A second was manhandling my breasts with one hand; I felt the face of the third, who had lifted my shirt from behind, press against my buns, very near to my little hole, something rude like horsehair that passed between my thighs and rummaged about on the front side; I reached down with my hand; what did I grab? the beard of Father Hilaire, who, feeling himself caught and pulled up on by the beard, gave me, to make me release him, a rather strong bite in the ass. I let go, in effect, of the beard, and let out a piercing cry, because of the pain, which fortunately for me made these unbridled beasts release me from their paws. I sat down on a couch that was near me; but as soon as I felt myself recovering what do I see but three enormous tools pointed at me.

"Ah! my Fathers," I exclaimed, "some patience please, if you don't mind; let's put a little order in what remains for us to do. I didn't come here to play the vestal virgin: let's see then, which one of you three should I..."

"Me!" cried out all three of them at once, without giving me a chance to finish.

"You, young barbarians?" took up one of them, speaking with a nasal twang. "You dare dispute first place with Father Ange, former guardian of..., preacher of Lent at..., your superior! Where is your sense of subordination?"

"My faith! we're at Dupuis's place," rejoined one of the others, in the same tone; "here Father Anselme is the same as Father Ange."

"You lie!" replied the latter priest shouting and brandishing his fist in the face of the Very Reverend Father Anselme. This latter, who was no weakling, jumped on Father Ange; the two went at it, grabbed each other by the throat, fell backwards, shredded each other with their beautiful teeth; their robes, pulled up over their heads, uncovered their miserable tools, which, from the salient beasts they had shown themselves to be, now were reduced to wet dishrags. Dupuis ran to try and separate them; she succeeded finally by throwing a large bucket of fresh water on the shameful parts of these two disciples of Saint Francis.

During the fight, Father Hilaire showed little interest in the tussle. As I had fallen back onto the couch, lying on my back, chuckling with laughter and without any strength, he rummaged over my charms and tried eating the oyster which his two companions were in the process of smashing their faces over; he cracked open the shell halfway, but there was no place to enter. What to do? He tried again to penetrate: lost efforts, useless endeavors. His tool, after redoubled efforts, was reduced to the humiliating expedient of spitting into the face of the oyster that he could not swallow.

Calm returned suddenly to the two monastic

furies. Father Hilaire asked for a moment of silence; he informed the two combatants of my irregularity and the insurmountable barrier that blocked entrance to the sojourn of pleasure. Old Dupuis was reproached with heated words, which she fended off by joking, and, like a woman who knows the world she operates in, she tried diverting them with the arrival of a convoy of bottles of Burgundy that were immediately uncorked and drunk.

Meanwhile, our Fathers' tools regained their previous consistency. Bacchic libations were interrupted from time to time by libations to Priapus. As imperfect as they were, our licentious monks seemed to enjoy themselves, and sometimes my buttocks, sometimes the reverse side, acted as altars to their offerings.

Soon an excessive gaiety seized everyone's mind. We put rouge and beauty marks on our guests: each one of them was decked out with one or another of my feminine accoutrements; little by little I was stripped completely naked and covered in a simple Capuchin coat; they found me charming in my new gear. "Aren't you so happy," cried out Dubois, who was half-drunk, "to have the pleasure of seeing the cute little face of someone as charming as Manon?"

"No, by golly!" replied Father Ange in a tone of Bacchic furor; "I didn't come here to see a cute little face: I came here to fuck a cunt is what I did; I have paid dearly," he added, "and these sons of bitches I brought along with me'll leave, by God! without having fucked so much as the Devil!"

"Now listen to this," Bois-Laurier said to me then, interrupting herself; "it's quite original; but I warn you (maybe a little too late) that I can't mince terms, without making the story lose some of its character."

Bois-Laurier had begun the story too elegantly to leave it hanging: I smiled; she continued the recitation of her adventure thus:

"Not so much as the Devil," repeated Dupuis quietly at first, getting up from her seat and raising her voice with a nasal intonation, in imitation of the Capuchin; "Well! bitch," she said, yanking her skirts up to her navel, "look at this piece of pussy... Venerable; it's worth two of the Devil's; I'm a she-Devil myself: fuck me, then, if you dare, fuck me for all your money's worth." As she said this, she pulled Father Ange by the beard and drew him close to her, pulling him down with her as she fell onto the bed. The Father was not at all disconcerted by his Proserpina's enthusiasm; he pulled out his peter and entered her right there and then.

The sixty-year-old Dupuis had barely felt the friction of several pushes by the Father when a delicious pleasure, that no mortal had had the audacity to make her enjoy for more than twenty-five years, transports her and makes her immediately change her tune.

"Ah! my father," she said, thrashing about like a madwoman, "my dear, dear father, fuck me then; make me happy! gimme all you got!... I'm only fifteen years old, my friend; yes, can't you see? I'm no more than fifteen years old... Aren't you excited? Push then, my little Cherub!... you make me feel alive... you're doing meritorious work..."

In the intervals between these tender exclamations, Dupuis kissed her champion, she pinched him, she bit him with the two teeth remaining in her head.

For his part, the Father, who had really drunk too much wine, could only plod along as best he could; but, with this wine starting to take effect, in the gallery, composed of the two reverend Fathers Anselme and Hiliare and myself, we quickly saw that Father Ange was losing speed and that his movements stopped being regular. "Ah! you bastard!" cried out suddenly the expert Dupuis, "I believe you're getting soft on me..., dog; if you insult me like that!" At just that moment, the Father's stomach, upset by the agitation, vomited, and the inundation, going straight into the face of the unfortunate Dupuis, while she was making one of her amorous exclamations, with her mouth wide-open, – she got a mouthful. The old woman, feeling infected by this vile libation in reverse, felt her own stomach churning, and she paid the aggressor in kind.

Never has a more awful and laughable scene been seen to occur at one and the same time. The monk grew heavier and collapsed on to Dupuis; she made heroic efforts to roll him off her; she succeeded. Both of them were wallowing in filth: their faces unrecognizable; Dupuis, whose anger had been merely suspended, laid into Father Ange with her fists; my immoderate laughter and that of the two other spectators took away our strength, and we were unable to run to his rescue; finally we reached them and separated the two champions. Father Ange had fallen asleep; Dupuis cleaned herself up; by the time night had fallen, each one of her guests had retired tranquilly to his home.

After this wonderful story, which prepared us for laughing our heads off, Bois-Laurier continued more or less in the following way:

I haven't told you at all of the bent some monsters have whose only pleasure is in unnatural acts, either as agents, or passively. Italy produces fewer of them today than France does. Haven't we heard about a rich, amiable lord who, infatuated by this frenzy, could not consummate his marriage with his charming bride, the first night of their honeymoon, except by having his valet, who was ordered by the master, while he was in the heat of the act, to fuck him in the ass while he was fucking his wife in the vagina!

I point out however that these unnatural gentlemen laugh at our insults and strongly defend their predilection, maintaining that their antagonists conduct themselves according to their same principles.

"We are all looking for pleasure," these heretics say, "wherever we think we might find it. Our adversaries are guided by their inclinations, so are we. Now, you will agree that we are not the masters of such and such an inclination. But, some people say, when pleasures are criminal, when they outrage nature, one must reject them. Not at all; as far as pleasure is concerned, why not follow one's inclination? No one is guilty of a crime. Besides, it is false to say that what is unnatural is against nature, because it is the same nature that gives us the penchant for this pleasure. But, they continue, one cannot procreate. What pitiable reasoning! Where are the men, of one or the other persuasion, who take pleasure in the flesh with a view to making babies?"

Finally, continued Bois-Laurier, these unnatural gentlemen allege a thousand good reasons to make you believe they are not to be pitied nor blamed. Whatever it might be, I detest them, and I have to tell you a story of a trick I played once in my life on one of these execrable enemies of our sex.

I had been warned that he was going to come visit me; and although I am naturally a frequent farter, I took the precaution of filling my stomach with a large quantity of turnips, so as to be in a better position to receive him according to my plans. He was an animal whom I would not suffer if it weren't in order to please my mother. Each time he came to our lodgings, he spent two hours of his time examining my buttocks, opening them, closing them, putting a finger in the hole, where he would have gladly attempted to insert something else, if I hadn't read him the riot act; in a word, I detested him. He arrives at nine o'clock in the evening; has me lie down flat on my stomach on the edge of the bed; then, after having carefully lifted my skirts and my shirt, he proceeds, according to his commendable practice, to arm himself with a candle, with the design of examining the object of his worship. That's where I was waiting for him. He put a knee on the ground and, bringing the light and his nose close, I let one, at point-blank, a smooth wind that I had been keeping inside me for nearly two hours; the captive, escaping, made an enraged sound and dropped his candle, which went out. The curious man jumped backwards, while grimacing, doubtless, like all the demons in hell. The candle that had fallen out of his hand was lit again; I took advantage of the confusion and escaped, while busting out in laughter, to the next room, where I locked myself in, and from which room neither prayers, nor threats could make me draw the bolt from the door, until my snubbed man had left the house.

Here, Madame Bois-Laurier was obliged to stop her narrative because of my immoderate laughter. Good companion that she was, she laughed with me wholeheartedly: and I believe that we would have continued to go on laughing if it wasn't for the arrival of two gentlemen of her acquaintance who had just been announced. She had just enough time to tell me that this interruption peeved her immensely, in that she had only had the time to tell me the bad part of her story, which could only have given me a very bad impression of her, but that she hoped to be able to acquaint me with the good part of it as well and to inform me with what eagerness she had seized the first opportunity that presented itself to be extricated from the abominable way of life that Lefort had engaged her in.

I must, in fact, do Bois-Laurier some justice; if I except my adventure with M. R***, which she had never wanted to be involved in, her conduct has been aboveboard for as long as I've known her. Five or six people made up her small circle of friends: I was the only woman she saw, and she hated them otherwise. Our conversations were decent before all the world: nothing so libertine as those we held in private since our reciprocal confidences. The men she saw were all sensible people. They dabbled in little business ventures, then they dined at her place almost every night. Only B***, that fake uncle the financier of hers was allowed to converse with her in private.

I said that two gentlemen had been announced; they entered; we played a game of quadrille, we supped gaily. Bois-Laurier, who was in a particularly charming mood, and who was perhaps concerned lest I be left alone to my thoughts after my adventure in the morning, pulled me to her bed. I had to sleep with her: when in Rome, do as the Romans do; we said and did all sorts of crazy things.

My dear count, it was on the day following that libertine night that I spoke with you for the first time. Happy day! Without you, without your advice, without the tender friendship and happy affinity that bound us together from the start, I would have gone to ruin without realizing it. It was a Friday: you were, it's coming back to me now, sitting in the amphitheater of the Opera, almost right below the loge where we were seated, Bois-Laurier and I.

If our eyes had crossed by chance, they would have fixed on each other. One of your friends, who was supposed to be one of our guests that same evening, joined us; you approached him after a while. I was being teased about my principles of morality; you seemed curious to know more, and then you were charmed into getting fully acquainted with them. The similarity of your feelings to mine attracted my attention. I listened to you, I saw you with a pleasure that I had not experienced before. The liveliness of that pleasure animated me, made me spirited, developed in me feelings that I had not perceived before.

Such is the effect of the mutual feeling of our hearts: it seems that one thinks via the organ of the person by whom one's heart is moved. When I said to Bois-Laurier that she should invite you to sup with us, you made the same proposition to your friend. Everything clicked; the Opera finished, all four of us mounted your carriage which carried us to your small furnished residence, where, after a game of quadrille which we paid for through the nose because we were so distracted, we went to a restaurant, sat down at the table, and we supped. Finally, if I regretted seeing you go, I felt pleasantly consoled by the permission you had asked to come and see me sometime, with a tone of voice that convinced me that you were serious.

When you had left, the curious Bois-Laurier questioned me and tried to get to the bottom of the nature of the particular conversation that we had had, you and me, after supper. I told her quite naturally that you appeared desirous of knowing what kind of business had brought me to and kept me in Paris, and I owned that your manners had inspired me with enough confidence that I didn't hesitate to inform you nearly of the entire story of my life and the present state that I found myself in. I continued to tell her that you had appeared to me touched by my present state, and that you had made me understand that, afterwards, you would be able to give me proof of the feelings that I had inspired in you.

"You don't know men," Bois-Laurier told me; "for the most part they're seducers and liars, who, after having taken advantage of a girl's credulousness, abandon her to her fate. It's not that I've this idea of the count's character personally; on the contrary, everything indicates that he's a thoughtful man, an honest man, who is this way by reason, taste, and prejudice."

After several other discourses by Bois-Laurier, whose intention was specifically to teach me how to understand and recognize men's different characters, we went to bed; and, as we were in bed, our craziness got the better of our reason.

The following morning, Bois-Laurier said to me, as she was getting up: "Yesterday I told you, my dear Thérèse, pretty much all the miseries of my life; you've seen the bad side of the coin; now have the patience to hear me out: you'll get to know the good side."

"A long time ago," she continued, "my heart was racked with remorse, and I complained about my unjust and humiliating life, which poverty had plunged me into, and where the habits and advice of Lefort retained me, when this woman, who had the art of holding over me a kind of mother's authority, fell ill and died. Everyone believing me to be her daughter, I quietly became the inheritor of all she possessed. I found, between the cold cash and the furniture, the china, and the linen, a sum total of nearly thirty-six thousand *livres*; keeping only for myself what was absolutely necessary, in the same way as you see me living today, I sold the remainder, and in the space of a month I arranged my affairs, so that I was assured a lifetime annuity of three thousand four hundred *livres.* I gave a thousand *livres* to the poor, and departed for Dijon, with a plan to retire and spend tranquilly the rest of my days there.

Along the way, I was taken ill with smallpox at Auxerre; it so changed my features and my face that I became unrecognizable. This event, combined with the poor care I had received during my illness, in the province that I had proposed to inhabit, made me change my mind. I also understood that, returning to Paris and staying away from the two quarters that I had lived in during my first two stints there, I could easily live in a third, without being recognized. I returned one year ago. M. B*** is the only man who knows me for who I am; he wants me to call him his niece, for I pass for a woman of quality. You are also, Thérèse, the only woman whom I've confided in, persuaded as I am that a person who has principles such as your own is incapable of abusing the trust of a friend you have become attached to, by the goodness of your character and by the equity that reigns in your feelings.

Continuation of the Story of Theresa the Philosopher

When Madame Bois-Laurier had finished, I assured her that she could count on my discretion, and I thanked her from the bottom of my heart that she had overcome, in my favor, the repugnance that one naturally feels when informing someone of the dissoluteness in her past.

It was about noon at that time. We were exchanging our usual polite remarks to one another, Bois-Laurier and I, when someone announced that you had come to see me. My heart leapt for joy; I got up, I ran to you; we dined and spent the rest of the day together.

Three weeks flew by, so to speak, without our being able to quit each other's side, and without my having noticed that you were using this time to understand whether I was worthy of you. In effect, drunk with the pleasure of seeing you, my soul felt no other feeling inside me; and although I had no other desire than to hold on to you for the rest of my life, it never once dawned on me to devise a plan to assure me of this happiness.

However, the modesty of your expression and the wisdom of your procedures with me never ceased to alarm me. If he loved me, I told myself, he would have the same lively behavior that I see in such and such other men, which assures me that they are head over heels in love with me. That disquieted me. I was ignorant at that time that rational people love in rational ways, and that thoughtless people are always thoughtless.

Finally, my dear count, at the end of a month, you told me one day rather laconically that my situation had disquieted you from the first day you met me; that my face, my character, my confidence in you had made you decide to find the means by which to draw me away from the labyrinth I was about to enter into. "I must appear quite cold to you, mademoiselle, quite distant," you said, "for a man who assures you that he loves you. However, there is nothing more certain; rest assured that the passion affecting me the most is the one that will make you happy." I wanted to interrupt you at that moment to thank you. "Now is not the time, mademoiselle," you resumed; "you must hear me out. I have twelve thousand livres in annuities; I can, without any inconvenience to myself, provide you with two thousand of them throughout your life. I am a bachelor, with the firm resolution never to marry, and determined to quit high society, whose bizarreness begins to take too much of a toll on me, in order to retire to a rather beautiful piece of land that I own that is forty leagues from Paris. I plan to leave in four days. Do you want to accompany me as a friend? Perhaps, subsequently, you will decide to live with me as my mistress: that will depend on the pleasure you will have to give me; but be assured that this decision will only work if you yourself feel that the relationship contributes to your own happiness.

"It is madness," you added, "to think that a man can make oneself happy merely by his way of thinking. It has been proven that one does not think as one wants. To be happy, each person must seize the type of pleasure that suits him, that is suitable to the passions he is affected by, while combining what results from the good and bad of the enjoyment of this pleasure, and observing that this good and bad should be considered not only in terms of oneself, but in terms of public interest. It is a given that, – just as man, by the multiplicity of his needs, cannot be happy without the help of an infinite number of other people, – everyone must be careful not to do anything that might harm his neighbor's felicity. He who distances himself from this system runs away from the happiness he seeks. Whence one can conclude with certainty that the first principle each person must follow to live happily in this world is to be honest and observe human laws, which are like the bonds of society's mutual needs.

"It is evident, I say, that anyone who deviates from this principle cannot be happy; they are persecuted by the rigor of the laws, by remorse, and by the hatred and contempt of their fellow citizens.

"Reflect then, mademoiselle," you continued, "on everything that I have just now had the honor of telling you: consult your heart, see if you can be happy by making me happy. I leave you now; tomorrow I will return to have your response."

Your discourse had shaken me. I felt an indescribable joy imagining that I had something to contribute to a man who thought like you do. I perceived at the same time the labyrinth I was about to enter and how your generosity might save me from it. I loved you; but how powerful are our prejudices and how difficult it is to destroy them! The idea of being a kept woman, which I had always attached a certain amount of shame to, made me shiver. I feared also becoming pregnant. Both my mother and Madame C*** had barely escaped dying in childbirth. Moreover, the habit I was in to procure for myself a kind of sexual delight that I had heard was equal to what we receive in the embraces of a man retarded the fire of my sexual appetite, and I never had any desire in this sense, because my desires were quenched immediately. It was only, then, the perspective of impending poverty or the desire to make myself happy, by making you happy, that could decide me. The first just grazed me; the second is what decided me.

With what impatience I waited for your return, from the moment you left! The following day you appeared; I rushed into your arms. "Yes, sir, I'm yours," I cried; "be considerate of the affection of a girl who cherishes you: your feelings assure me that you'll never constrain my own. You know my fears, my weaknesses, my habits. Give your advice some time to sink in. You know the human heart, the power our feelings have over our will; use your advantages to make blossom in me the feelings you believe are the most suitable for making me contribute unreservedly to your pleasure. In the meantime, I'll be your friend, etc..."

I remember that you interrupted me during that sweet, heartfelt effusion of mine. You promised me that you would never constrain my tastes nor my inclinations. Everything was settled. I broached my happiness to Bois-Laurier, who broke out in tears as we separated, and you and I departed finally for your lands, on the day you had fixed.

Once arrived at this darling place of sojourn, I was not surprised by the change in my condition, because my mind was occupied only with the care of pleasing you.

Two months passed without your pressuring me on the desires you sought to bring out unconsciously in me. I exceeded all your expectations of pleasures, except sexual pleasures, whose raptures you spoke highly of to me, but which I didn't find to be any greater than what I normally felt, and that I was offering to share with you. I shuddered, on the contrary, at the sight of the shaft you menaced piercing me with. How could it be possible, I said to myself, that something so long and so fat with so monstrous a head could be received into a space that I could barely slip my finger into? What's more, if I became pregnant, I feel, I would die. "Ah! no, my dear friend," I continued, "let's steer clear of that fatal reef; leave it to me." I caressed, I kissed what you called your doctor; I performed some moves on it that, by robbing you of that divine essence, in spite of yourself, brought you to rapture and reestablished the calm in your soul.

I noticed that, as soon as the goadings of the flesh had been blunted, under the pretext of the enjoyment I took in talking about morality and metaphysics, you used the force of your reason to lead my will where you liked.

"Self-esteem," you said to me one day, "is what decides all the actions in our lives. What I mean by self-esteem is the internal satisfaction that we feel when we do one thing or another. I love you, for example, because I find pleasure in loving you. What I do for you might be agreeable to you, might be good for you; but you are certainly not obliged in any way. Self-esteem is what decided me: it is because I fixed my happiness on contributing to yours; and it is for this same reason that you will make me perfectly happy only at such time as when your self-esteem finds its own happiness thereby. A man often gives alms to the poor, he goes out of his way even to assist them: his action is useful for the good of society; it is praiseworthy in this sense; but, as far as he himself is concerned, there is nothing more to it than that. He gave alms because the compassion he felt for those unfortunate people excited in him a painful thought, and he found it less disagreeable to part with his money in their favor than to continue to endure the pain excited by his compassion; or perhaps even that his self-esteem, flattered by the vanity to pass for a charitable man, is the honest-to-goodness interior satisfaction that decided him. All our actions in life are guided by two principles: to procure more or less pleasure for ourselves, to avoid more or less suffering."

On other occasions, you explained things to me, you expanded on the short lessons that I had received by the abbot T*** "He taught you," you told me, "that we are no more in control of what we think, or of our will, than whether we should decide to have a fever or not. In fact," you added, "we see by simple and clear observations that the soul is mistress of nothing, that it acts merely in consequence to the feelings or the faculties of the body; that the things that might produce a disturbance in our organs trouble the soul, alter the mind; that a blood vessel or a fiber upset in the brain can make a man stupid to the world around him which has greater intelligence. We know that nature acts only according to a uniform principle; now, as it is evident that we are not free in certain actions, we are not free in any. Let us add to that that if our souls were purely spiritual, they would all be the same; if they had the faculty of thinking and willing on their own, they would think and act in the same way under the same circumstances; but that is not what happens; so they are influenced by some other thing, and this other thing can be none other than matter, because the most credulous among us admits of only mind and matter.

"But let's ask these credulous men what mind is. Can it exist but not be anywhere? If it is somewhere, it must occupy space; if it occupies space, it has an extent; if it has an extent, it has sides, and if it has sides, it is matter. So the mind is a chimera, or it is a part of matter.

"From this reasoning," you said, "one may conclude with certainty, firstly that we think in such and such a way only with respect to the organization of our bodies, combined with the ideas we receive daily by touch, sound, sight, smell, and taste; secondly that our life's happiness or unhappiness depends on this modification of matter and these ideas; that it is in this way that geniuses, the people who think, cannot overdo it in terms of the cares and troubles they cause themselves as they come up with ideas that might efficaciously contribute to the public good, and particularly to the people whom they love. And so ought mothers and fathers to act with respect to their children, governors and administrators with respect to the people, teachers with respect to their students!"

Finally, my dear count, you began to grow tired of my refusals, when you had the brilliant idea of having transported here for me, from Paris, your books of amorous literature and your paintings in the same genre. The pleasure that I showed for books, and even more so for paintings, made you imagine two means by which to succeed in your endeavors. "You love then, mademoiselle Thérèse," you said to me jokingly, "amorous literature and paintings? I am delighted: you will have the most outstanding representatives; but let us make an pact, if you do not mind: I consent to loan to you and have placed in your room my library of books and my paintings for one year, on condition that you promise for two weeks to place not so much as one finger on that part of your body that, by right, ought today to belong to me, and that you make a clean break from masturbation. No quarter," you added. "It is fair that each of us put a bit of 'skin in the game.' I have good reasons for demanding this from you: you decide; without this commitment though, no books, and no paintings."

I had no hesitation, I made a vow of continence for two weeks. "And that is not all," you then said to me: "let us impose on ourselves reciprocal conditions: it is not fair that you should make such a sacrifice for a momentary view of paintings and reading of books. We will make a wager, which you will doubtless win. I will wager my library and paintings, for your virginity, – that you will not observe continence for two weeks, as you have promised."

"In all honesty, sir," I responded to you, somewhat piqued, "you've quite a strange idea of my sexual desire, and you think I'm not in control of myself!"

"Oh! mademoiselle," you replied, "no arguments, I beg you. You make me unhappy. I feel, moreover, that you have not guessed the purpose of my proposition: listen to me. Is it not true that each time I give you a present, your self-esteem is wounded to receive it from a man whom you do not make as happy as he could be? Well! the library and the paintings, that you love so much, will not make you blush, for I will not have given them to you, – you will have earned them."

"My dear count," I responded, "you're setting a trap for me; but you'll be the dupe, I warn you. I accept the wager!" I exclaimed, "and I give you my word, what's more, to occupy myself every morning with nothing more than reading your books and looking at your charming paintings."

Everything was brought to my room on your orders. I devoured with my eyes, or, it might be more accurate to say, I read through one after the other, during the first four days, of *The Story of the Charterhouse Porter*, that of the *Carmelite Extern Nun*,

The Academy of Ladies, *Ecclesiastical Laurels*, *Thémidore*, *Frétillon*, *A Woman of Pleasure*, *Aretino*,[18] etc., and a number of other titles of this kind, that I couldn't put down except to examine with avidity the paintings in which the most lascivious poses were rendered with a coloring and with an expression that kindled a burning fire in my veins.

On the fifth day, after an hour of reading, I fell into a kind of ecstasy. Lying on my bed, with the bed curtains opened on all sides, two paintings, *The Celebrations of Priapus*, and *The Love Making of Mars and Venus*,[19] gave me some perspective. With my imagination warmed by the attitudes that were depicted there, I threw off the sheets and blanket, and, without reflecting whether the door to my room was

---

[18]Original footnote: We have to believe that certain titles figuring in this list were added after the appearance of the first edition, or that the first edition itself appeared later than we believe: *Story of Don B****, *The Charterhouse Porter* (by J.-Ch. Gervaise de Latouche), 1745. – *The Story of the Carmelite Extern Nun*, in response to P. of the C. (perhaps Querlon), 1745. – *The Academy of Ladies*, *or the Seven Amorous Conversations of Heloise*, 1680. – It's a translation, or rather adaptation, of the famous Latin work by Nicolas Chorier, who is also called "Meursius." – *The Ecclesiastical Laurels or the Abbot T***'s Companions* (by the knight de la Morlière), 1747. – *Thémidor* (by Godard d'Aucourt), 1745. – *The Story of Mademoiselle Cronel, Nicknamed Frétillon* (by Gaillard de la Bataille), 1739. – *Memoirs of a Woman of Pleasure, or, Fanny Hill*, 1751. – It's one of the first translations [from the English] of the libertine masterpiece by John Cleland. – *Aretino, or The Debauchery of the Mind as an Act of Good Sense* (by the abbot du Laurens), 1763.

[19]*The Love Makings of Venus and Mars*: Possibly a reference to *Venus and Mars Surprised by Vulcan*, by Joachim Wtewael; or to (although less likely because less steamy) *Venus and Mars* by Sandro Botticelli.

closed or not, I went about imitating each of the poses that I saw. Each figure inspired in me the feeling that the painter had given to it. Two athletes who were on the left side of *The Celebrations of Priapus* enchanted me, transported me, by making the pleasure of the little woman in the painting my own. Without thinking, I moved my right hand to that place on my body where the man's was placed, and I was on the verge of inserting my finger, when a thought held me back. I became aware of the illusion, and the memory of the conditions of our wager obliged me to stop.

How far from my mind was the thought that you were a spectator to my weaknesses, if this sweet penchant of our nature should be called a weakness, and how crazy it felt, good God! to resist the inexpressible pleasures of a real enjoyment! Such are the effects of prejudice: they blind us, they are our tyrants. The other parts of this first painting excited first my admiration and then my pity. Finally, I cast my eyes on the second one. What lasciviousness in Venus' bearing! Like her, I extended my body limply. My thighs a bit apart, my arms voluptuously open, I admired the brilliant attitude of the god Mars. The fire with which his eyes, and principally his lance, appeared to be animated touched my heart. I touched myself, arching my back and lifting my hips up off the sheets, my buns agitating voluptuously, as if to offer the crown destined for the conqueror.

"What the devil!" I cried, "the divinities themselves take their happiness from an act I refuse to partake in! Ah! dear lover, I can no longer resist! Where are you, count, I'm no longer afraid of your prick:

you can enter your lover now: you can even choose where you want to strike: it's all the same to me; I'll suffer your blows with constancy, without murmuring; and to assure you of your triumph, here you go, my finger inserted!"

What a surprise! what a happy moment! You appeared in the flesh, all of a sudden, more proud, more brilliant, than Mars himself in the painting. The light dressing gown that you were wearing was removed. "I had too much delicacy," you said to me, "to take advantage of the first opportunity you gave me: I was at the door, where I saw everything, heard everything; but I did not want to owe my happiness to the winning of a clever wager. I came, my lovely Thérèse, only because you called me. Are you decided?"

"Yes, my dear love!" I cried out, "I'm all yours! strike me, while the anvil is hot, I no longer fear your blows."

At this moment, you fell into my arms; I seized, without hesitation, your shaft which until then had appeared so redoubtable to me, and I positioned it myself at the opening that it threatened; you pushed in, without causing me the least cry by your redoubled blows: my attention, fixed on the idea of sexual pleasure, didn't allow me to perceive any pain.

Already, rapture seemed to have banished the philosophy of the man, master of himself, when you said to me with ill-articulated sounds: "I will not use, Thérèse, all the right I have acquired: you are afraid of becoming pregnant, I will go easy on you; the moment of pleasure is upon me; put your hand again on your conqueror; when I take it out, help me, by your touch, to... It is time, my girl; I... am... in... ecs...tasy..."

"Ah! I'm dying too," I shouted, "I cannot feel myself anymore, I... am... swoo... ning!..." Meanwhile, I had taken your prick, I squeezed it gently in my hand, which served as its holder, and in which it came. We did it again, and again, and our pleasures were renewed, for ten years, in the same way, everyday, without any trouble, without children, without worry.

There you have it, I think, my dear benefactor, what you insisted that I write of the details of my life. How many sots, if ever this manuscript should come to light, would decry its lasciviousness, would denounce the principles of morality and metaphysics that it contains! I will answer these sots, these lumbering machines, these kinds of automaton, accustomed to thinking by someone else's brain, who avoid doing such and such a thing because someone told them not to, I will tell them, I say, that everything I have written here is based on rational thought detached from any prejudice.

Yes, ignoramuses, nature is a chimera. All is God's work. It's from him that we have the desire to eat, drink, and enjoy all pleasures. Why blush then while fulfilling his designs? Why fear to contribute to the happiness of other humans, by teaching them these various ragouts, designed to satisfy through sensuality their diverse appetites? Shall I be afraid to displease God and men by announcing truths that can only enlighten them without harm? I say it again, atrabilious censors, we do not think as we want to. The soul has no will, it is determined only by feelings, by matter. Reasoning clarifies things for us; but it does not decide us. Self-esteem, pleasure expected, or displeasure to be avoided, are the reason behind all our determinations. Human happiness depends on the conformation of our organs, education, external feelings; human laws are such that man cannot be happy except by observing them, by living as an honest man. There is a God; we must love him, because he's a supremely good and perfect being. The sensible man, the philosopher, must contribute to the public weal by practicing regularity in his mores. There is no worship, no religion at all, God is sufficient unto himself; the genuflections, the imaginings of men cannot augment his glory. There is no moral good or bad, except in relation to God. If one person is physically harmed by something, another person derives benefit; the doctor, the public prosecutor, the financier, live off the harm done to others: it is all one system. The established laws in each region must be respected; anyone who breaks them must be punished, because, as the examples restrain men who are poorly organized, who have difficulty controlling themselves, and who have bad intentions, it is just and right that the infractor's punishment should contribute to the general peace of society. Finally, kings, princes, magistrates, all the various superiors, by gradations, who fulfill the duties of their state, must be loved and respected, because each one of them contributes to the good of society.

The Carmelite Extern Nun

Saint Nitouche, the Amorous True Story of the Carmelite Extern Nun Written by Herself, and Addressed to Sister Geneviéve, Mother Superior of the Salpêtrière Hospital

Anne-Gabriel Meusnier de Querlon

A Letter from M.T*** to M.D***

No, sir, the Carmelite Extern Nun, whom you have spent so much of your time researching to no avail, is not a rational being: this work, written to serve as a counterpart to the *Charterhouse Porter*, has been in existence for three or four years now, but it has not exited the hands of its author, with whom I'm on good terms. The title of it is *Saint Nitouche*, or *The Carmelite Extern Nun, A True Story, Written by Herself, and Addressed to Sister Geneviéve, Mother Superior of the Salpêtrière Hospital.*[20] The manuscript that I saw can be made into a small folio in 12s.[21] The work is written in a pure and more elevated style than that of Dom B.,[22] and although it is as libertine as the latter book, even though it is for the most part the story of a bawdy house, there is not a single obscene or gross word in it; I will say nothing about the author, who is my particular friend and whose person and name will remain an inviolable secret with me, except to say that he is quite above this misery, as he calls it. It is a short, witty sketch that he made for his own

[20]Salpêtrière: Pitié-Salpêtrière Hospital, in Paris, was a hospital for the insane, but also a kind of prison for prostitutes, the poor, and women who were mentally ill or disabled.

[21]folio in 12s: duodecimo format. In other words a small format book made of twelve leaves per sheet (or folium).

[22]Dom B.: *The Charterhouse Porter.*

amusement, & an attempt to see, from what he told me, just how far licentiousness may be taken, without mentioning any obscene words or phrases: which is, in my opinion, a condemnation of all our modern idiots; there was never any plan while writing this work – to *publish* it (which is pointless to expect) – but merely to show it, for it was not without a great deal of effort that I persuaded him to let me see it, & that I was able to obtain a copy of it to read. It is true that I could read it at my leisure at his home, on two or three occasions; but it was only after a month, after pestering him about it, that he allowed me to make a copy of it, which I did as he looked on; I made the most complete copy I could. Given that he placed no conditions on me about this morsel, I agree to make it available to you; it will give you at the very least an exact idea of the entire work. You will see the intention, the genius, the conduct, you might even judge the style, and the author's manner of writing, by some of the main extracts from the novel that I took pains to represent here.

I have the honor, &c.

In Versailles this...

Dedicatory Epistle to Sister Geneviéve

My Very Dear Sister,

The edifying Lives of the Saints are not always the most useful; it is good to have before one's eyes models of virtue in order to follow them; but it is no less important to see some scenes or paintings of vice in order to conceive of the horror in them. Full of this principal, which I have experimented in, I had the most singular idea that a young girl could think of, & that is to write down my story. By the grace of Providence, I find myself, after all my distractions, in a peaceful place of refuge where I now have all the leisure in the world to go back over, with vivid regrets in heart and mind, every moment of my voluptuous youth. Completely devoted previously to the impure pleasures of the public,[23] and now of no more use to the world, I thought I ought to work towards other peoples' instruction; I will hide nothing of the circumstances of my former life, I want to show myself for what I was, and my soul will stand naked before the world. I will blush doubtless myself, from all the excesses I will describe; but I must not spare myself this salutary confusion, and the more forceful and true the depiction of my lubricious life appears, the more useful I imagine it will be for me, first of all, &

[23]the public: in other words, she was a "public" woman, viz., a prostitute.

then for others. If one finds that I have not properly engaged the imagination of the reader, I have at least respected my own eyes and ears; that is all that is asked of me today, & provided that the objects be veiled, the gauze is never too thin, even as regards our fairer sex. Besides, there is something about this naïve story that is similar to an infinity of other books wherein all the danger consists only in the disposition of those who read it. As for me, in the my current state of penitence, I owe it to myself this kind of public confession. I beg my readers to consider it with all the simplicity of intention that I had when writing it, & it is in this same spirit, my dear Sister, that I took the liberty of dedicating this writing to you.

I am with a deep respect, my Very Dear Sister, your very humble & very obedient servant,

Agnes P***.

The Carmelite Extern Nun's Tale

My birth announced what I would be one day, & what I am; what I wish to say here is, my taste for pleasure, & my vocation for retreat; my mother, who was born of highly decent parents, but of mediocre fortune, the youngest of three Sisters, was extremely pretty, & at an age of seventeen when the idea of becoming a religious was the furthest thing from her mind, the family made arrangements for her to take the veil with the Ursulines in the City of N***. She was not consulted, neither her feelings nor her temperament, about this decision. She was extremely surprised, it was as if a glass of cold water had been thrown on her while she was sleeping, & if they had so much as bothered to examine her disposition and personality, they would have seen that *everything* inside her protested against the violence of this decision; she was no longer mistress then of her inclinations, & a young man in the neighborhood was in complete possession of a thoroughly profane heart, which her parents had decided to devote to God, in spite of themselves. One can easily see what might follow from this forced engagement.

Sister Radegonde suffered from a malady of languor, that exhausted all the science of the doctors, who could do nothing for her, & which led her to the brink of the grave; they were at their wit's ends as to what to do for her when one doctor from Paris prescribed as a last resort the thermal baths at Forges-les-

Eaux.[24] They were all the more willing to go out of their way not to refuse her this assistance given that the prioress of the house where she lived, who was crippled in a part of her body, was condemned to making the trip for a long time now.

Radegonde's lover, who had always continued an exchange of letters with her, was alerted and didn't fail to meet her in route. They made their way to Forges-les-Eaux together, at an easy and leisurely pace, & their frequent meetings were more efficacious than the waters; Sister Radegonde was healed, & the prioress hauled her bones back to the convent.

My mother (the Historianess resumes) who, after having tasted love's first fruits with her beau Duvilly, and having longed for them all the more intensely, found herself inconsolable by their separation, & mulled over a thousand ways to leave the convent, until she found a consoler more energetic than her lover was. Father Arlot, a vigorous Mathurin,[25] aged 40, had replaced Father Colard, who had been out of commission for a year already. Pretty soon he got to the bottom of Sister Radegonde, and understood her sexual desire, which he resolved to profit from. The loves of Radegonde and the Mathurin: My mother (continues the Extern Nun) didn't stop there. The house gardener, a big rustic boy, but who was more promising than Father Arlot, seemed suitable to fill her void, which the needs of some of the other sis-

[24]Forges-les-Eaux, in Normandy, a spa town, with thermal waters, popular from the sixteenth century onwards.

[25]Mathurin: a member of the Trinitarian Order based out of the church of Saint-Mathurin in Paris.

ters and the good Mathurin's charity made inevitable; & she helped herself amply.

I was conceived over the course of these divers incidents because my mother started showing signs of pregnancy six weeks after her return from Forges-les-Eaux; so that it was not clear who my natural father was: Duvilly, Father Arlot, or the Gardener. Whatever the case, I am the issue of one of the three, unless one wants to give me three fathers: I don't follow in my mother's footsteps in any way, shape, or form; there's no question here of anything but me, &c.

Sister Radegonde gave birth. The child was reckoned to be Mathurin's, who felt himself obliged in all good conscience to provide for its future, & made arrangements with the prioress.

Agnes (that's the name of the Extern Nun) is handed over to a wet nurse. Paternal cares assumed by Father Arlot. Agnes' primary education. At ten years old, a decision is made to have the child breathe her natal air, & she enters the convent of her mother as her niece. Portrait of Agnes.

Nature, she says, had formed my face in a most deceitful way, & made it all the more suitable to hide all sorts of excess of vice under the appearance of virtue. My face, which displayed an air of candor and modesty, without my even trying, would have passed me off for an angel, & I was called Saint Nitouche,[26] which name I have since held on to; & I confess that it is the only trait I retained from my days in the convent.

My mother's offense was forgotten, everything had been conducted in great secrecy: she gradually assumed more and more responsibility over the house, and I was seen as a girl one wished to instill a taste for the convent in.

Saint Nitouche wears the secular habit for two years: in her third year, she uncovers the secret of her birth. Father Arlot had retired, & turned over the cares of the daughter to the mother who was now prioress. New intrigue for Radegonde with the chaplain of the house, a big seminarian, who had succeeded the Mathurin.

I was curious (said the Extern Nun) what she was doing so often with the chaplain in the guest hall; & as curiosity has always gotten the best of me, I hid myself one day, with the intention of spying on her, under a table covered by a large cloth. The prioress and the chaplain didn't take long to appear. A padded wing chair of the most comfortable kind served as the backdrop for their sexual pleasure. Soon, I saw the holy man in the posture of the Prophet Elisha resuscitating the widow's child.[27]

"Do be careful, dear friend," she said, "let's not spoil things by our imprudence, it's already cost me dearly...." Upon saying which, the chaplain

[26]Saint Nitouche: originally it was "saint n'y touche." It refers to someone (primarily a female) who affects simplicity and innocence.

stopped; he wanted her to explain what he already knew quite a lot about: she fended him off for a time, & finally she gave in and recounted to him her weakness for Duvilly, and the entire adventure at Forges-les-Eaux. She was going to follow it up with her story about her love affair with Father Arlot; but the chaplain had heard it all before from that religious, & anticipated her by telling her a number of anecdotes she barely remembered. He added that he had taken over Father Arlot's place in the confessional. "But Father Arlot," he continued, "was a bit jealous of your gardener friend: what I don't know is what happened between you two. You owe me the truth in this tribunal of love even more so than in the tribunal of penance."

My mother confessed to M. Adam what she had made Mazette do, and they resumed their intercourse from earlier. My mother, while exhorting the priest to be careful, shook him fervidly, and they made her wing chair rock, crack, and bend. M. Adam wanted to pull out; at this moment I saw my mother hold on to him vigorously & made, in order to hold him, a double chain of her arms passed around his neck & her legs intertwined with his. She said to him in a dying voice, "No, my dear, don't stop... Ah! more slowly... come then... quickly... come with me...." I hadn't the faintest idea what the Priest was doing, at least I was ignorant at this time? I describe what I saw, & what were for me my first ideas of love: I

[27]resuscitating the widow's child: Presumably 2 Kings 4 in the Bible. But one wonders whether the author is not conflating the widow and her two sons, which comes before it, with the story of the Shunammite woman whose son died and was restored to life. In any case, it is a salacious interpretation of the Old Testament tale.

made two important discoveries on that happy day, the one being that I was the daughter of the prioress whom until that time I took for my aunt; the other being how I had been brought into the world.

During this interesting scene, I was almost stimulated by the same movements as my mother was, at least I didn't miss a beat; & nothing escaped my eyes or my ears from where I sat under the covered table: the posture in which I found myself was a bit awkward, & I wanted to get more comfortable, in order to hear the continuation of their conversation; but by moving I made a noise that frightened the lovers, & our lovers froze with fear. My trembling mother urged the chaplain who was in a similar state as she was, to go look under the table, & they uncovered the ambush. Sister Radegonde's anxiety and perplexity. Friendly questions made to her daughter to understand what she had seen and heard. Naïve responses by Agnes in which one could see hints however of a little mischievousness, which prompted the chaplain to say to the mother: "Do you detect, dear Eve, the little mask? I wager that a seed from the apple we have eaten not a few times has already germinated in her heart, what do you say?" Radegonde's embarrassment; she was uncertain how to act with her daughter. After having considered the matter carefully, they concluded to let her in on the mystery; and the acknowledgement between mother and daughter took place in accordance with all the rules of the theatre.

Since that time, Agnes focused on trying to find the means to experience for herself the fruit that she had seen her mother eating. I had seen everything, Agnes said, postures, attitudes, & movements; but I was still far from my goal, & did my penetration into the matter take into account the differences between the sexes? Sometimes I slept with a girl about my same age, & was it enough for two girls to sleep together before they became inseparable? The arrival of new boarders cramped us for several days, & I had my bed companion. From the very first night together, I wanted to try what I saw my mother do; & because it seemed to me that my mother was the more excited of the two by the feelings of pleasure, without making any distinction between agent and patient, I had my good friend assume the priest's position, & I mimicked as best I could my mother. But after having warmed ourselves up pointlessly for more than an hour, without knowing even how to procure for ourselves the pleasure that two women can give one another; our enterprise's lack of success & the reflections that it gave us succeeded in shining a light on my stupidity.... There was a young boy who, for the last six months, was employed by the house to run errands in town, & he was free to enter the convent.

Little Michel (that's his name) came dressed rather properly and had a pretty face; and although he appeared but a child because of his little *wawa*, he was at least 15 or 16 years old.

It was on this champion that I set my sights, to enlist him in the services that M. Adam had rendered my mother. His young wawa didn't stop me at all from thinking that he would stand in for a man, having all the advantages of his sex; & is this what I asked him to do? He came and went freely anywhere he wanted; it was up to me to arrange the moment when we could find ourselves alone, & I found it soon enough.

Little Michel is approached by Agnes, who tries to instruct him: she makes him hard, & he botches it after two or three attempts? Finally by dint of trying all sorts of postures, he succeeds in taking her virginity. (The description of this, which was too long to transcribe, is one of the strongest passages in the work.) Little Michel's embarrassment at the sight of the blood that came out during the combat; they both begin crying.

This first attempt was too successful for them to stop there; their intercourse becomes more frequent, and soon they take so few precautions that one day they are surprised in the act by the depositary. Portrait of that old religious who hadn't always been so irreproachable herself, & who had even given birth to a child. She tells the funny story of her discovery of the two to the Mother Superior who recognizes her mark,[28] said the Historianess. The prioress has her daughter and Little Michel come before her, and after having interrogated them as to the facts and details, the boy is forbidden to enter the cloister. Our young lovers find a way to see each other in the tower of the sacristy, and finally they get so much of each other that Little Michel falls ill. Agnes' situation. His illness is attributed to their separation, and the good prioress consents to letting him see her dear Agnes again. The effects of this on the two lovers. Little

[28]mark: or hand in the matter. Possibly the mark of Cain?

Michel gets better, but Agnes succumbs to the first symptoms of another kind of malady, which is the fruit of their labors. The prioress notices her condition, & without so much as verifying it, she chases the boy away. Because Agnes' swelling gets to the point where she is unable to hide it any longer, despite all the precautions taken by her mother, she is made a pensioner in the house of a mid-wife, and she gives birth there secretly. A young surgeon, the nephew of the matron, discovers and sees Agnes by accident; they soon take a fancy to each other; & before Agnes has completely recovered, she engages in sex and is made pregnant again, unbeknownst to herself: and there she is looking like her old self again in face and figure, the rehabilitated daughter, so far as she knows; for the weakness she had for this new lover didn't seem to her to be of any consequence given she had just given birth to a child, and the young surgeon being a man of the profession had reassured her on his score. The prioress decides that it is time for her to return to the convent and to make her take the veil, completely resolved to watch over her so well that, even if she does have sexual desires, she would never find the opportunities to satisfy them; it was the only option she had; because left to shift for herself, what would Agnes do in the world, having no other patrimony to give her than her wimple & one of the most equivocal of vocations. At the end of two months at the cloister, Agnes falls victim to the same condition that Little Michel had gotten her into. Anxiety and perplexity on the part of the prioress, who notices it with the first symptoms, & who cannot imagine how with all the precautions she has taken, her daughter could have enjoyed for a second time the forbidden fruit. She puts the question to her, and the daughter confesses that her new pregnancy is a result of the time she spent at the mid-wife's, & that the mid-wife's nephew had made this miracle. The incident becomes more embarrassing than the first time because of the veil, but Agnes happily was only a novice: they pretend that she's disgusted with the convent, that she asks to reenter the world, and she's placed with the mid-wife who had taken the precaution of sending her nephew to Paris to deliver babies. After Agnes had given birth a second time and regained her strength, her mother, not knowing any longer what to do with her, sends her to Paris as an orphan, to a fiercely devout and wealthy aunt, whom she entrusts with both her destiny and her behavior. Agnes is received by the aunt and placed in the hands of her chambermaid as a subordinate, in order to prepare her to succeed her one day. Agnes' disgust for a position that appears to her much more difficult than she imagined, with a mistress her relative in whom she cannot confide. These feelings of rising up in the world are soon snuffed out by a more dominant passion: she falls in love with the little house lackey and becomes pregnant for the third time. On perceiving her pregnancy, the great aunt writes to her niece, with the expectation of sending Agnes back. Such a fecundity makes her mother shudder; but indulgent for her blood, by force of prayers, she obtains from the aunt a promise not to abandon Agnes on account of this accident.

The good aunt, touched by this orphan's fate, has her give birth outside the home; & as soon as she is restored to her former self the aunt places her in apprenticeship with a linen merchant at the palace, strongly advising the latter to watch over her charge. As soon as I arrived at the palace (said the Historianess), I stole all the hearts and took all the attention: all the other girls were abandoned, & I became the single object of coquetries by all the galant busybodies that chicanery or curiosity attracts. I was put on display in the middle of a brilliant boutique; nobles of the robe and of the sword came and went continually in order to reconnoitre the place and God knows how I was ogled. A young and galant clerk had the honor of matriculating me into the palace, & he was my first conquest at arms; but our commerce didn't last long. The linen maid who had been a little too easy in her day, and older now, was severe in proportion, and punished three of the girls, myself included, who were about the same age, for being younger than her. By the second or third day I was brought up to speed on the entirety of her life by one of my companions, who knew through the grape vine whom she had replaced, having learned about it from her predecessor. Our pedagogue was once famous among all the orders. The nobility of the sword and of the robe, the clergy, and the third estate had all shared moments with a youth usefully employed and extended even beyond the normal limits. All her austerity could not prevent me in the least from penetrating deeply within the hierarchy of clerkdom, and I made all the magistracy submit. The more I served love, the more it seemed to recompense me in the worship of my new charms: three pregnancies one after the other had only made me more beautiful. The linen maid, despite her scruples, had been rather indulgent until then, & had looked the other way when it came to my dissipations; but I exceeded all bounds, and in order to repress my coquetry, she resolved to confine me for a time in the backroom. I don't know if she was treating me like a rival or not, at any rate it's always the same with all older women who were once amorous. Besides, this one was a bit devout; a quality that ends up by making her look ridiculous: there I was condemned at the end of two months to the obscurity of the storeroom. The suitors dried up at the same time, the boutique became deserted, & sales plummeted with my eclipse. Personal gain finally opened my mistress' eyes, fixed on the clerks as they were; I always attracted some shopper. She came to her senses, & realizing her mistake, she resolved to put me on display again, come what may.

I reappeared after this short retirement which served to restore some of my old color, making me more attractive and prettier than ever. The same day I was reintegrated (forgive me for using this word, my dear mother, I speak the local tongue), the very same day then that I took up my place again in the boutique, the place was packed; young lawyers came by the dozens, and soon pushed out the clerks. Senators succeeded the lawyers. And no sooner was I ogled by the president of the court and was about to elevate myself to the high robe, when an old pillar of the palace, the dean of all the stewards in the world, made solid propositions and offered to set me up with my own place. I accepted without hesitation, for to be known as a kept woman meant a lot to me, and I had an agreeable idea of my position. So I left the linen boutique with no regrets, & I renounced all the honors that the palace had offered me in perspective, to have the pleasure of fleecing this dirty old man who had fleeced so many others before me.

Agnes lived for about six months in such good relations with the royal steward, and for a first try at this she hauled in quite a lot; the most experienced theater girl would have done no better. Honestly, she said, on my own I would have been hard pressed to do as good as I did, & I profited enormously from the advice of a gendarme whom I had taken as a lover, & with whom I shared the liberalities of his old rival.

When Agnes' intrigue with the gendarme was discovered by the steward, the latter planned on dumping her & taking back all he had given to her. Instructed in his plans by the tapestry maker, whose palms she had greased, she anticipated the steward by packing up her clothes and things, changing neighborhood and name, & moving in with the gendarme. They lived quite happily together while the funds lasted, but unfortunately the gendarme gambled a little and drank a lot; Agnes herself loved to shop. After two months their strongbox was empty and that was the end of their secret relationship. The furniture and expensive clothing was sold little by little to subsist on, & disagreements between the lovers began to crop up in their life of misery together.

Finally Agnes was reduced to a single dress & had fallen into a state worse than what she had been pulled up out of by the steward, whereupon she was obliged to abandon the gendarme. When they separated he offered her disinterested advice, such as not attaching herself to anyone, stealing whatever she could lay her hands on, & putting herself above the weaknesses in her character that he himself had profited by.

Agnes, who found herself completely exposed now, was unfortunately hardly in a position to profit from this helpful advice, for she knew nothing yet about those accommodating women who charitably assist girls who are without hearth or home, as she was then. What to do in her extremity? She had been successful working as a linen maid; she found the means to enter into the service of a wholesale merchant of fashion on rue Saint Honoré, where there were cart loads of girls. Crowds of men passed by there, she said, old buzzards, white beaks,[29] young starlings, all the neighborhood birds of prey; but although my first thoughts in life had been to let my sexual desire take the upper hand, I began to wise up, & the poverty I found myself in made me realize the value of money which I had paid little attention to previously, when I was rolling in the dough. I let myself be taken in less by eye candy, & my idea was to fix my sights on some honest man of mature age, the kind of man who is the dupe of women, & not those lovable and handsome deceivers whom the greater part of women are the dupes of. I had in my crosshairs a fat treasurer who was approaching sixty years old, & who stopped by everyday to purchase some bagatelles in order to speak with me; he made me some propositions, but I showed too much re-

[29]white beaks: in the extended bird metaphor it is hard to find an exact match in English; dropping the metaphor, one might say here "smooth operators."

serve, or I haggled too much with him: the old man wasn't crazy about sighing for an overly long period of time, and one of my colleagues, who knew better how to close the deal, stepped in for me. This incident was a good lesson to me, but I pivoted too far in the other direction. I was always on the lookout, & I exaggerated the flirting to the point that my too great facility scared away a number of men who appeared at first to desire me. They thought I was more experienced than I was, & all that I gained at that boutique after two months of expectation & coquetry was to stir up some of the procuresses who thought I was right for putting their business back on a solid footing. Two of the more famous among them argued over my acquisition, & wanted to undress me before the eyes of the public in order to retail me. Each one took me aside and made me an offer, & I sided with the one who persuaded me the best, & learned her trade.

Here begins, my dear Sister, the miserable tissue of a life, a thousand flesh-and-blood examples of which live with you here at the convent.

There I was, Agnes the initiate, & a public woman. The good woman who produced her had her hands full with her adjustment, given she was in not too good a condition: she was not allowed to be seen by young men, and was introduced mysteriously as a young wife who cheated on her husband in spite of his vigilance. Soon, in this role, she found herself extremely busy, & made the gold flow abundantly into the patroness' coffers.

What a life, my dear Sister, she exclaimed!

What an agreeable condition! The object of new flames that one snuffs out and rekindles over and over again, the pleasures of the table and the boudoir succeeded one another or were confounded twenty times a day. What a charming state of affairs, if only it lasted! Because I had an extremely comely body, I was continually exposed to all the caprices of the imagination, to all the refinements of voluptuous behavior; & soon I had worn down all Clinchetel's pencils.[30]

I'm reminded of one fat prior, who to relieve his monstrous corpulence, came up with this expedient.[31] He made me lie completely naked on a trestle bed in my natural pose; two girls of the greatest suppleness that one could find were put under the bed, and by reiterated pushes with their back we produced a marvelous elasticity.

But there is no such thing as pure pleasures, and the most sensuous life is always intermixed with some disgraces.

One day five musketeers came in half-drunk to let loose and unwind in Agnes' little room. "At the time I was with," she said, "an unimposing tax farmer-general, whom by forced caresses I was able to empty the wallet of." A party of Hussars who surprise a convent of nuns cause them hardly any more alarm than this mischievous youth gives women of our profession. But this man, a peaceful and mature man, wanted to withdraw immediately. One muske-

[30]Clinchetel's pencils: Clinchetel was a painter of miniatures, whose real name was Klinastedt apparently.

[31]Original footnote: borrowed from Petronius.

teer grabbed him by the arm and said, far from wanting to interrupt his pleasures, that they came to share them with him, & that finally they wanted to drink with him. The bourgeois left them masters of the battlefield and prudently beat a retreat. Our scatterbrained men were now in possession of the place. As it was late and because it was just me and the patroness at that moment, I was on my own at the mercy of their petulance. They ordered a lot of wine to work themselves up to the task, and I was soon in their ardent crosshairs. Three of them, more worked up than the other two, grabbed me, & making me get stark naked on the bed, they took their positions: the first, to use the expressions of these libertines, was going to stage a frontal attack; the second, who was going to attack from the rear, put his miner to work; & the third countermined them both by inserting a siege instrument into my mouth; a fourth kept the beat in order to regulate their movements, so that all three discharged at the same time, & soon I was covered, from head to foot, with the sap that had been fermenting in them.

This new kind of debauchery gave me a taste for sought-out pleasures. I came up with several poses that earned me no small honor in the world, and that I don't have the vanity to describe here.

Everything was going along swimmingly until the point when our musketeers, after having drunk so much, and the night being quite advanced now, it was no longer possible to get rid of them. One of them, dead-drunk, falls vomiting in the middle of the room, & unable to move, falls asleep, lying in a pool of wine; another while fondling the patroness and pulling her down to the floor, because he wanted to take her virginity, so he said, was also surprised by sleep; a third stretched out on a wing chair snoring at the top of his lungs, with a glass in hand, filled with wine, spills it all over him; a fourth, after having warmed himself up with me, fell asleep in the act he was making such good progress at, and I had a devil of a time to roll him off me; finally the fifth worn out by trying to slap his comrades awake, fell asleep at the table. Imagine for yourself, if you can, this scene, worthy of the brush of Lafage.[32] As for the patroness and me, we passed the night half cursing the musketeers and half laughing at the figure they cut. Morning came, & the distributor of slaps who was the first to awaken, sounded the retreat, by turning everything upside down. His comrades awoke, & as soon as they became aware of their clothes and their hats soaked in the debris of their dinner, – this sight put them in a very bad mood; I couldn't help letting out an indiscreet laugh, which this frightening scene elicited from me, & I was paid immediately by an enormous slap across my face. The mistress of the lodging wanted to bring home to them gently the scandal of such impolite behavior, & she received two or three slaps herself. She was a fiery Picard, easy to lose her temper, & battle-hardened by such scenes. She couldn't remain without responding in kind, & immediately she seized a chair and threw it at the slapper. That did it. Soon the mirrors, the bed, the commode, the table and chairs were destroyed. Imprudently, I began to cry out the window for help; the lookout who was retiring

[32]Raymond Lafage, a seventeenth-century painter and sketcher.

now ran back toward the noise, forced open the door on the street and mounted the stairs: our five musketeers were politely asked to please go home and rest up from the fatigues of the night, & we were instead all escorted to the commissary of police, who had us sent to Saint Martin's, & a few days later we were led into your community. And that, my dear Sister, was the beginning of our acquaintance. I spent, on this first occasion, three months in such good company at your house, & I profited a lot from this retreat. I had promised myself to change the entire plan of my life, but it was a frivolous resolution. What change was I capable of? Accustomed as I was to the sweetness of an idle and sensuous life, the disgraces that accompanied it no longer frightened me, because of the experiences I had had; & I exited finally from your place a little more corrupted than when I entered it.

Agnes, before leaving the Salpêtrière, was approached by three famous procuresses she had made acquaintance with there. She reenters the world and sets herself up in the Faubourg Saint Germain; for the next five months, her public life is a succession of misery & prosperity. At one moment lifted well above her status, at the next moment reduced to the level of lackeys, she goes about under different names which she changes as often as her residences, all the amorous cubbyholes and hideouts in the faubourg, like a novice who, with a fleeting desire for the cloister, throws on a frock, and flies from convent to convent, unable to make up her mind. I never succeeded in attracting to myself, during all this time, continues Agnes, anything other than the small, ordinary godsends that are inseparable from our line of business.

But by dint of squandering my favors, I contracted a contagious form of syphilis that all the waters of the Jordan River would be unable to wash away; for all that, I deserved it, for a large number of women like myself who moaned about their condition only continued to work at it by necessity or habit. But sexual desire had the upper hand in my case: I never saw a handsome and well-built man who didn't excite me; & the number of those who, for lack of choice, stood in for them, always filled my heart well enough. Nature must have endowed me with a marvelous fund of feeling, that it should never be appeased or blunted, as I have noticed in quite a number of girls who, though much younger than myself, had much less practice.

One day in a celebrated atelier where I had set myself up just the night before, a well-dressed man with a kind expression on his face arrived, who, after having reviewed the entire community of courtesans, stopped and confided in me his utter surprise at seeing me there. I got the handkerchief, & when we were alone, he asked me a hundred questions about my birth, status, and place of origin.

I thought he was a procurer, as we call these gentlemen, & on this basis I told him all sorts of lies that could be useful, without hiding the truths that I thought could be of some advantage. Among other things, he asked me one question in particular that caught me off guard, – he asked me if I didn't have an aunt, who was a nun, in Province; I thought this might give me some distinction, and I confessed to him that yes, I did in fact have an aunt among the Ursulines in

N*** whom I resembled quite a bit. He asked me for news, but I didn't know what to say, & I began crying. He added that he had known her in his youth, & that they had met at Forges-les-Eaux at the start of his profession. I viewed him more favorably after this admission; I remembered Duvilly & the entire conversation between my mother and the chaplain. I no longer had any doubt that this knight was none other than the hero of the story I had overheard, & I discovered my mother had really good taste in men. However, in order not to waste time in useless explanations that moved me and renewed my remorse with each passing moment, I changed the conversation on a dime, & I went about practicing my profession dutifully. I had no trouble getting him into the mood. This beginning of our acquaintance, although couched in obscurity by me, gave him no small satisfaction in me: he wanted to spend the night, & gave me his order for supper. A thousand other scruples then shook me; I was extremely sad at the table, in spite of caresses and each guest's gaiety. A lack of clarity as to my origin and the large role he had played in it, & the suspicion of his paternity, which my mind gloated over however with secret satisfaction, empoisoned in advance every sweetness that his nearness promised me; the adventure had to be cut short. I went to bed, completely irresolute as to how to play my hand, & I was about to slam on the brakes before his burning desires, when my cruel sexual desire came to his rescue. He had barely made his advances, when I went well and beyond his expectations, & I embraced him with a passion that I had never felt before. If Nature made me feel some stirrings at that time, they were confounded with those of love. And (I say this with horror) perhaps alas! they actually augmented the intensity. It got warm in my room, and we took off all our clothes. How gentle and sweet my dear father was, if it's possible he was my father even; he kissed every inch of my body a thousand times, & a thousand times my lips passed over his. Forgive me, Sister Geneviéve, a little weakness I have, there are just a few more strokes of the brush to go. I know of no other way to depict with such candor and intensity a crime for which I should blush. O Mirrha! whatever idea we might have from the fable of your desire for the handsome Cinyras, it cannot come close to what I felt. After having plunged into a torrent of delights, importunate remorse followed. Alas! in exchange for the pleasure that Duvilly gave me, I gave him a fatal present in return; the venom flowed with the honey. I prepared the cruelest thorns for him on a bed of roses, & the poison that I distilled for him had a much more profound impression as it was seasoned by intense delight. The night, which passed quickly, was well employed, when a softening of the light outside the windows announced morning. Duvilly woke early, & as he was pressed to get on with his day, he embraced me by way of saying *adieu*, when all of a sudden I was struck by an unusual idea. I put on a muslin dress that one of my companions wore as a nun's habit; I added the wimple and the veil, and like this, throwing my arms around his neck, I held him amorously in my arms. He found me pretty in this masquerade and was struck even more forcefully still than the night before by the resemblance that he found in me of my mother, and I saw with secret delight the complete effect that this thought had on him. In this habit, I wanted him to prove his love for me one more time, but he seemed to stand back in horror. I threw myself at him, & having pulled him onto the bed by caresses, I led him to my goal. I enjoyed at that moment, so it seems to me, more pleasure than the night before, & I noticed that his imagination had played its part admirably. We separated quite satisfied with one another, with promises to renew the game. I had no idea what would result from this amorous adventure, but two days later I was picked up by edict of the King.

A young man, fifteen or sixteen years old, the son of a businessman, who had seen Agnes three or four times, & with whom he had shared the fruits of her amorous labors, was obliged to confess to his family where he had come by that contagious windfall he was suffering from; & having indicated Agnes' name, address, and profession, by edict of the King she was ordered to be put in at the hospital. However, as I was in a certain state (she said) before inhaling the air of that salutary place of rest, it was necessary to pass through the probatic pool,[33] and they sent me at first to Bictêre.[34] A picture of that awful place. A description of what followed after the syphilis.

I had never yet reflected on, continued Agnes, any of the events in my life; but I didn't deplore my plight at all when I saw myself mixed up, under the

[33]probatic pool: not unlike the Pool of Bethseda, from a story in the New Testament, in which Jesus heals a paralytic man in its waters.

[34]Bicêtre: an orphanage, prison, lunatic asylum, and hospital, successively and simultaneously, in Paris.

arches, with the vilest of prostitutes. I saw them paying a bitter tribute for the pleasures they had given, for the most part without even sharing in the enjoyment as I had, & maybe I was the more guilty or the more justly punished. On departure from Bictêre, where she had stayed three months, Agnes was transferred to the Salpêtrière, and although she was in a familiar place, she disliked it more than the first time, & made a serious resolution to change her life. When the period of her penitence expires, she seeks the means to enter the order of the Grey Sisters,[35] succeeds in her ambition, & tries on the habit.

For six months of sojourn in this community she attaches herself to one very kind sister, who was the bastard daughter of Fillon; soon they become lovers and mistresses. The latter nun fortifies the distance Agnes seemed to put at that time between herself and all men in general, & from the world (conversation on this subject, wherein we can see a mixture of both devotion and libertinism).

Agnes, having become a tribade & an extreme tribade at that, believes she has forgotten men altogether, when a young priest assigned to her as her confessor falls in love with her. Their frequent interviews at the confessional restore her little by little to her taste for the opposite sex, she grows warmer day by day to his company, & having confided her weakness to the priest, he immediately effects her conversion. This new male lover of hers, fearing a relapse, has her quit the order of the Grey Sisters, and sets her up with a room; she's a kept woman again; they live

[35]Grey Sisters: the Daughters of Charity of Saint Vincent de Paul.

together rather peaceably for several months: she associates only with deeply religious people & is one of them herself. These liaisons lead her to strike up acquaintances with the Convulsionaries. A little widow initiated in the faith for six months grows fond of Agnes, but Agnes' spiritual director and beau unfortunately was a Molinist; the Convulsionairy undertakes to detach her and succeeds, she gives her a Jansenist for a lover, and soon she becomes a Convulsionairy herself.

Pleasant digressions on convulsions, descriptions of several scenes that serve as a cover for libertinism, Agnes becomes famous under the name of Sister Pétronille. Adventures that happen to her. Someone comes to arrest her, she escapes. This incident coupled with the discredit into which the Convulsionaries have fallen, makes her disgusted with this type of life; she makes a resolution to reintegrate with the world and find a profession. She leaves her Jansenist lover and moves out without saying a word. She associates with an old friend from secondary school, and they open a house of prostitution together, sharing the startup costs. The beginnings of their business are not brilliant, they needed to start by limiting themselves at first to domestics, but they lift themselves up little by little to target bourgeois clientele. She wanders about in this way assuming different names in the more lively neighborhoods of Paris, changing lodgings every two or three months; finally, having developed a taste for business, she separates from her partner with the intention of running her own house & working for herself. She furnishes a place based on the money she has amassed and establishes herself. Her reputation and her good conduct allow her to acquire in no time a brilliant house. She had seven or eight girls, top tier in terms of youth and beauty, not to mention married women who came to work for her. She had to register with the police captain of the precinct who was one of her lodgers, and two exempts who took bribes, and used their influence on the investigation officer. I had put, she said, on the books an admirable police officer, & I had small, very comfortable apartments, offices, open spaces, hidden stairways, nothing was missing. I received very few military types and youths, unless it was the son of the Treasury Department official, whose good behavior I was familiar with, but lots of lawyers and magistrates and central government officials, good fathers of family, fat merchants. Above all, I had a ton of ecclesiastics, that is to say, very few seminarians or none at all, for they are almost as mutinous as musketeers, but also good priests, and a number of canons; as for monks, I received few Cordeliers (they are rowdy), but Jacobins, members of the Premonstratensian, Victorin, and Celestin orders, &c.

I also provided for some tax farmers-general, & a good number of Our Lords of the Clergy. Oh! how many maidenheads I sold, restored, and sold again for the tenth time more dearly than the first. How many girls, after ten years of service, done over and employed as new, I would have passed off as passionate Furies, for a piece of Prince! How many married women whose taste for simple pleasures contributed even more to enlarge the tribute that I siphoned off the public, and who after having shared with me the work and fatigues of the day, went home and generously left their honorariums to me. (Story of la Duchapt, the famous merchant of fashions.)

In this way, I steered my little boat marvelously, and I was on the verge of expanding beyond Paris, to Maupoint, to Florence, when an accident turned my fortune upside down. I was living with an officer of the militia, who was a Protestant himself, & who took me under his wing. His only fault was getting drunk and acting a bit brutal when he was in his cups, otherwise he was the best child in the world; & provided one left him alone at the table, he could be led around like a sheep. One day I was visited by some young men who were sent by a prostitute whom I had previously corrupted handsomely. I was alone in my room with an old, very rich notary, & who paid like an English lord for only a little amusement. They were a regiment of two or three companies. At first, I tried to refuse them entry, but they pushed the domestic out of the way, and took over the place: we were only women at the time (no bouncers). Two honest ecclesiastics, the one a director of a community and the other a famous preacher, were barged in on and escaped on first sight of these libertines. The petulant cohort was at first shocked that they should have been refused entry; I threatened to call the police captain. The words had barely escaped my mouth, when they began attacking my furniture and belongings, & they aimed at destroying everything they could lay their hands on; threats, entreaties, caresses, nothing could stop these madmen. One of these brutes in response to some representations I wanted to make, because he was removing my mirrors from the wall, turned his fury against me and pounded my face in. My poor officer of the militia, led by his unlucky star, arrived in the middle of all this disaster; & as he was not the strongest of men, despite the condition he saw me in, he took it upon himself to attempt conciliation: they threatened to throw him out the window, with my furniture which began to take this route. After some harassment, he drew his sword and wounded a young man, immediately three more fell upon him and left him stretched out on the floor: now the whole building and neighborhood were up in arms. What to do in this extremity? I thought only of my safety at this point, I took with me what money I had, & I escaped in the midst of that tumult: the police captain and archers came & talked with them.

I don't know anymore what became of this affair, after having gone into hiding for two months at the periphery of Faubourg Saint Jacques. Disfigured as I was, I was fortunate enough to make the acquaintance of some of the devout followers in the quarter, & I begged them to help me find an honest place of retreat; they practiced with the Carmelites, & proposed that I enter in the capacity as an extern nun. They were looking for one, & my badly beaten face, acting as a security for my good behavior, didn't frighten at all these good daughters of Christ. And this is where, after nearly forty-five years, I spend my days tranquilly, & where I give to God what remains of a life that is of little use to the world. In all honesty, my dear sister, you could never recognize me at all, alas! the only thing I regret is my face; the springtime of my life is over, I have to confess, but in my wildest dreams I could not have expected my career to have ended so suddenly.

THE END

Other Books by the Publisher

Fanchette's Pretty Little Foot
by Restif de La Bretonne

Je M'Accuse...
by Léon Bloy

My Hospitals & My Prisons
by Paul Verlaine

Salvation Through the Jews
by Léon Bloy

Words of a Demolitions Contractor
by Léon Bloy

Cellulely
by Paul Verlaine

Flowers of Bitumen
by Émile Goudeau

Songs for Her & Odes in Her Honor
by Paul Verlaine

On Huysmans' Tomb
by Léon Bloy

Ten Years a Bohemian
by Émile Goudeau

The Soul of Napoleon
by Léon Bloy

Other Books by the Publisher (cont.)

Blood of the Poor
by Léon Bloy